The Rifle Captain

A Novel of World War I

W. Steven Harrell

PublishAmerica

PublishAmerica
Baltimore

First printing

ISBN: 1-4137-0607-X
PUBLISHED BY PUBLISHAMERICA, LLLP
www.publishamerica.com
Baltimore

Printed in the United States of America

*This book is dedicated to my
beautiful young daughters, Sally and Marian.
And to my son Alex, who is always loved,
and who will never be forgotten.*

CHAPTER ONE

The rolling hills of North Georgia were beautiful in the spring of 1917. Stephen Harris was up early in the morning , before daylight, gathering eggs from the chicken coop for breakfast. He then walked over to the barn and milked Daisy, his large Jersey cow. Daisy swished her tail at him a time or two as he milked her.

At six a.m., still in his overalls, he delivered the raw milk and fresh eggs to his lovely and devoted wife, Loralie, a buxom green eyed beauty. She is dressed in an apron and a smock, with her honey colored hair pinned back in a bun.

Loralie had bacon frying in a skillet on the wood stove, and she began to prepare eggs for breakfast as her biscuits baked in the oven. She reminded Stephen to wake their little girls, and to see that they were dressed for school.

He walked down the hall to check on Millie, his six year old blonde haired blue eyed girl, and he sees her buckling on her shoes by her bed. The bed was made, and her room was orderly and neat.

He checked across the hall for Annie, their eight year old daughter, and sees that she has finished dressing as well. He then called the girls to breakfast, and grace was said quickly, and then they began to eat hastily. Stephen poured strong coffee for Loralie into her cup, and then complimented her on her delicious breakfast.

He continues to be amazed that she would marry him. He met her at a Baptist Church social near Royston twelve years before, and he immediately knew that she was his one soulmate. He told her many times that all she had to do was bat her pretty green eyes at him, and he would move mountains for her.

They married six months later, after a whirlwind courtship. They came to live on his mother's farm that he had inherited from his parents in 1905. Stephen's father was killed in action with Teddy Roosevelt's Rough Riders on the San Juan Heights in 1898. His mother, Estelle Harris, died of Scarlet Fever in 1905.

Her one hundred acre farm was devised to him, and they moved into the farm house on Black Snake Road shortly thereafter.

Stephen's father had left him a sizable estate, and Stephen pursued his college education at the University of Georgia in Athens. He is employed as a professor of history at the Franklin County High School. Stephen and Loralie rented out most of the farm to a neighbor, Ned Sanders, who ran a dairy farm up the road.

Stephen finished his breakfast quietly, kissed Loralie on the cheek, and hurried over to their bedroom to change his clothes. He donned a tweed suit and waistcoat and a black tie, and remembered to gather his lecture notes on the War of 1812 on his dresser.

He walked back into the kitchen, and reminded the girls that they were late for school. He kissed Loralie good bye while the girls rounded up their school books. He walked out to the barn, and then hitched his horse, Cherokee, to a small buggy. The girls ran out to the barn, fetching Stephen his lecture notes. He gave them a boost up to the front seat of the buggy, and then mounted the seat himself. He clucked to Cherokee, and they moved out up the Black Snake Road. It is springtime, and the oak trees and hickory trees are beginning to bud out with new green leaves.

The rolling hills north and west of Royston were nothing less than beautiful, and even more so the spring of the year.

They passed a large field near Ned Sanders' dairy, and they waved at his son, Carl, who was driving the Holstein cows back into another pasture for the day. The girls were amazed that the cows had worn a path in the field between the milking house and their pasture. Freckled faced Millie had a question:

"Pa, why do all those cows wear out a path like that in the pasture?"

Stephen flicked the reins onto Cherokee's rump to make him trot a little faster. "That is from their daily habits. They are milked at least twice per day, and their mothers and grandmothers were driven back and forth the same way. That path has been there for years."

Annie lost no chance to question her father even more. "Is that where you found the arrow heads, Pa?"

"Yes child, I found most of my arrow heads over in that pasture

6

when I was a boy."

They crossed a covered bridge over the North Fork of the Broad River, a beautiful swift moving stream. Stephen made a mental note to himself that he would go fishing for trout that weekend just above the bridge at a large pool nearby.

They rounded a bend in the road, where a red one room schoolhouse stood. The school teacher, Irene Sanford, was out in her long skirt and her straw hat, showing a young boy how to pull the rope to ring the school bell.

Stephen spied small groups of children walking toward the school house. Stephen stopped the buggy, and helped Millie and Annie down. He handed them their books and lunch buckets, kissed them good-bye, and waved to Miss Irene.

He flicked the reins and clucked to Cherokee, who broke out into a faster trot on the road to Carnesville. They made a turn onto the paved highway, and soon, Cherokee was trotting into town, and the Franklin County High School building. Stephen pulled the buggy around to a barn at the rear of the building, where he was met by a fifty five year old Negro man in overalls.

"Good mornin' 'Fessor Harris."

"Good morning, Clarence. I believe Cherokee could use a pat down and some oats and water."

"Yes, suh, I'll attend to him right now."

Stephen handed Clarence a dime for his trouble, and then took his lecture notes and walked over to the high school building.

He walked down the hall of the large brick school building across the hardwood floors, and down to his classroom, Room 102. He switched on the electric lights in the classroom and at his desk, and opened his textbook to the lesson on the War of 1812. He then started copying terms, and writing notes on the blackboard behind his oak desk.

He wrote words on the blackboard that related to the day's lesson:

"HMS Leopard 1809"

"USS Chesapeake"

"Congress- War Hawks"

"John C. Calhoun"
"Henry Clay"
"Freedom of the Seas"
"Impressment"
"Blockade by Royal Navy"

Several minutes later, the students began to file into the classroom, saying "good morning Professor" as they passed Stephen at his desk. He nodded his head in acknowledgment as they passed. Boys dressed in linen and cotton shirts, tweed trousers with suspenders, some in denim bib overalls. Young ladies were also enrolled in his class, as his class was a required course over on the girl's side of the high school. The young ladies were dressed in long skirts with cotton or linen blouses, and some wore straw hats.

Most of the girls were tenth and eleventh graders, with their dark and their blonde hair pinned back in buns, like their mothers' hairstyles.

When the monitor in the hall rang the bell for classes to commence, Stephen rose from his desk. He was six feet two inches tall, weighed two hundred and twenty pounds, and had dark hair and hazel eyes. He tucked his railroad watch into his waistcoat, and began to speak clearly, in a baritone voice.

"Please take out your textbooks, and turn to page 225. Your assigned reading for today covers the War of 1812, and the reasons for the United States' involvement in the war. In 1809, the HMS *Leopard*, a frigate in the Royal Navy fired on, and her sailors boarded the USS *Chesapeake*. Why did they do this, Mr. Freeman?"

Robert Freeman was a sandy haired eleventh grade farm boy that Stephen called on to lead off the class, because he was always prepared. He stood up and addressed the class.

"The British impressed sailors on all U.S. ships whenever they got the opportunity. In the case of the *Leopard*, her captain took the position that British sailors were on board the *Chesapeake*. The captain of the *Chesapeake* had refused to allow the British sailors to board his vessel."

"Very good, Mister Freeman, you are correct. Impressment was the issue of the day. During the wars with Napoleon, British press gangs were constantly on the move, ashore and on the seas, impressing men into King George's service. The Articles of War were read to them once they were brought aboard a King's ship, and they could not desert under penalty of death.

"The Royal Navy's constant need for manpower and sailors fueled this policy and this practice of press gangs, but it had bad results in America. Who were the 'War Hawks'? Mr. Guest?"

A tall young man in tweed breaches and a linen shirt began to stand up. He pulled on his suspenders as he rested his arms.

"Henry Clay of Kentucky, and John C. Calhoun of South Carolina, they wanted the Congress to declare war on Great Britain."

"Very good, Judson. Mr. Guest, why was President Madison initially opposed to war with Great Britain?"

"Uh, because they had the largest navy in the world?"

"That is correct. England at that time had deployed over two hundred ships of the line, or battleships, and had over three hundred frigates, or cruisers, in the Royal Navy. They also had countless brigs, bomb vessels, and other smaller ships. With a navy that size, the American coast could be blockaded, and New England's shipping would be bottled up. His reservations about war were more than valid. Miss Hunter, what did Congress eventually do?"

A tall, willowy young woman stood up by her desk, and began to stammer. "They ... declared war on Britain, sir."

"Yes, they did, Miss Hunter. What was the issue that led the Congress to vote a declaration of war against Great Britain?"

"I'm sorry ... Mr. Harris. I am just not prepared."

Stephen dealt with that situation at once.

"See me after Mrs. Jenkins' Physics class this afternoon, Miss Hunter. You will get an extra assignment of reading from me today."

The blonde haired girl took her seat, and Stephen continued his lecture.

"The issue then, ladies and gentleman, was freedom of the seas. The President and the Congress then were concerned about British ships wrongfully impressing U.S. sailors into King George's service against their will. At stake was the sovereignty of a young United States. I have a more difficult question for you: How does this issue compare to our present situation with Imperial Germany? I will answer that one myself. We study history because it has a tendency to repeat itself. Just as in the War of 1812, a European power has threatened our freedom of the seas."

Stephen took out a folded sheet of paper from his coat pocket, and began to read.

"Two years ago, an Imperial German U-Boat sank the S.S. *Lusitania*, and hundreds of Americans were drowned. On February 25th of this year, a German U-Boat sank a Cunard liner *Laconia*, drowning four Americans. One week later, an American steamship *Algonquin* was sunk by a German submarine without warning, in an area that was previously designated as a safety zone.

"On March 21st, a U.S. tanker, the *Healdton*, was sunk by a German U-Boat without warning while in Dutch waters. This area was also supposed to have been a safety zone.

"President Wilson called Congress into special session on April 2nd, and asked for a declaration of war against Imperial Germany. Last week, on April 4th, the Senate voted in favor of war by 82 votes to 6. On April 6th, the House of Representatives voted to declare war on Germany by a vote of 373 to 50.

"Ladies and gentleman, we are at war with the Central Powers, since all of their member nations have a mutual aid treaty with Imperial Germany."

Stephen folded the piece of paper, and put it back into the pocket of his tweed coat.

"We have gone to war because our right to navigate the seas freely has been threatened. God bless the United States, and may we prevail on the battlefields in France, and around the world."

A monitor out in the hall rang a hand bell, indicating that the class period had concluded.

"Don't forget to read the next two chapters on the War of 1812. We will review some of the land and sea battles of the war this week.

Class is dismissed."

The students nodded in his direction as they left their seats and filed out of his classroom. Stephen wiped his brow with his handkerchief, and wondered how many of his history students would die over on the battlefields in France.

He made his way to his desk, and began to prepare for his World History class which would meet that afternoon. He began to study his materials on the Napoleonic Wars, and the sailing ships of the Royal Navy. In writing out his lecture notes, Stephen could not take his mind off the slaughter of the World War raging in the battlefields across the Atlantic. What was to become of him?

He knew that if he was called to serve, that he would report and do his duty. He opened a drawer in his desk, and took out a life insurance policy application. It was sent to him by an agent with the Metropolitan Life Insurance Company in Athens. He completed the application, wrote out a check for the initial premium, and placed the check and the application in the return envelope to mail back to the agent in Athens. He would consult his attorney in Carnesville about preparing a will next week, he thought to himself. It was high time that he got his house in order.

He then walked down the street to Helen's diner, where he normally ate her lunch special. Her special scrawled on her small slate board was meatloaf and green beans, for 50 cents. He took a seat in a booth next to the counter, where a tall blonde haired woman of forty two years came up to greet him. She was dressed in a long cotton smock, which covered a dark blue cotton dress, and she had her hair pulled back in a bun and tucked under a cotton cap.

"Hello Stephen. We have iced tea today. The ice truck brought us some ice this morning. Would you like some?"

"Yes Miss Helen, and I would like your special today also. Do you have any corn bread?"

"I just made some a few minutes ago. I'll bring you a piece with your meal."

"Thank you, ma'am."

Right after his iced tea was brought out, a tall, dark haired man of forty five years walked up and greeted Stephen.

"Hello, Sheriff Crawford. I was gonna look you up today, but you saved me the trouble. Please sit down a spell. I need to talk to you."

"Sure, I came here for lunch anyway." He was dressed in a gray suit with a white felt wide brim hat, and his brass Sheriff's star was pinned on the outside of his waistcoat.

The Sheriff waved over a fifteen year old girl who worked there as a waitress, and ordered the daily special and an iced tea.

"What did you want to talk to me about, Steve? Is Claude May sellin' moonshine at your high school baseball games again?"

"No, Sheriff, at least not lately. Congress has declared war on Germany, and I believe that a lot of men around here are gonna be drafted into the army. In fact, I believe that you are on the Draft Board that will meet next month."

"I am. So is Robert Freeman at the funeral home, and Mack Guest over at the Merchant's Bank. Bob Snow in Royston will also be on the Draft Board."

"This is what I was going to tell you, Sheriff ..."

Their plates of food arrived, and Stephen thanked the young waitress that brought out their iced tea and their plates.

"As I was saying, Ned Sanders served with my father in Cuba. He was first sergeant of dad's company. He said dad took a direct hit from artillery posted on San Juan Heights. When the regiment overran the Spanish positions, Ned told me that he inspected the guns. The artillery that killed dad were Krupp made German weapons. I owe the Germans something. If we are gonna get drafted, I want to already have a commission. You got some pull with Governor Slayton. I have trained many young men from this county. I am the best damn shot in this county. I can read topographical maps. I want a commission as a first lieutenant in the National Guard. If you wrote a letter to Governor Slayton, I think I could get that commission."

"I am proud that you would ask me, Steve. I believe I can speak for the entire Draft Board, and tell you that we would be honored to have you command a company of local boys. But just remember, the Army will require you to complete an Officer's Training Camp if you are called to active service."

"I understand. I will pay my dues, Sheriff. I just want a chance to really do some good over in France."

"I understand, son. Your dad was a special man. I promise you that I will write a letter to Governor Slayton when I get back to the office. I will even have the whole Draft Board sign it at our next meeting."

"Thank you, Sheriff. I really appreciate what you can do for me."

"We appreciate what you do for Franklin County, son. Just go out and win your varsity game tomorrow."

After lunch, Stephen taught his World History class that met at 1:30. The topic was the Napoleonic Wars. He began the lesson with Wellington and the start of the Peninsula Campaign, and concluded the lesson with Nelson and Trafalgar. He gave reading assignments which covered the next two chapters, and he handed out special reading materials concerning British ships of war and the Age of Sail. At two thirty, class was dismissed, and he stayed at the school for another hour to write out his lecture notes for his morning American History class. He used some of his notes from his Age of Sail materials for his lecture on the sea battle between the U.S.S. *Constitution* and the HMS *Java*.

He then packed up his notes, and walked down the hall to Principal Gregory Brown's office.

The principal had furnished his office with beautiful lamps, a horsehair sofa and chair, and a Red Oak desk in the outer office. A black haired beauty of twenty years, Sheila McRae, sat as the school secretary. She greeted Stephen in her usual flirtatious way, with a gleam in her eye. She was wearing a pastel blue dress, a mother of pearl broach, and a straw hat.

"Hello, Professor Harris. You look very nice today. Would you like to see Mr. Brown? He's in the office right now. He just got back from the baseball field."

"Sure, Miss McRae. I would like to see him for just a moment."

She rose from her desk slowly, to give him a good profile of her curvaceous body. She turned her head and spoke slowly.

"Oh, *do* call me Sheila, professor. All of my friends do."

"I will make note of that."

She stuck her head into the door and announced to Mr. Brown that Stephen had come to see him. She then pulled her head out of his office and spoke to Stephen directly.

"He said you can come right on in."

"Thank you, Sheila."

She rolled her pretty blue eyes at him as he walked past her. He thought about any single man that would attempt to court her, and he knew that the preacher's son had dated her. That boy sure had his hands full, he thought, as he entered the principal's office.

A fat man of fifty years stood up from behind his mahogany desk, dressed in a navy blue three piece suit. His gold watch fob was visible on his waist coat pocket.

"Stephen, my boy. What, no baseball practice today?"

"We'll dress early tomorrow and take infield practice before the game. I just wanted to talk to you about a couple of things before the game."

"Claude isn't selling white lightning out there again, is he?"

"No sir, it's not about that. I asked the Sheriff to write a letter to Governor Slayton today for me. I'm seeking a lieutenant's commission in the National Guard."

"Why, Stephen, aren't you happy here?"

"Of course I am, but I figure that I'll be drafted into the Army anyway. I would rather have a commission, if it can be arranged beforehand."

"I see. Well, I just got appointed to the Draft Board. I'll gladly sign any letter that Sheriff Crawford writes for you."

"Thank you, Mister Brown. I really would appreciate that."

"Oh, by the way, your new baseball uniforms are in at the dry goods store up the street. I'll send Sheila after them for you first thing in the morning. I'll lay them out on a table in the gymnasium. The boys can pick them up there after first period class."

"I'll announce it in all of the home rooms tomorrow. Thank you, Sir."

"Good afternoon, Stephen. Try to win another game for us tomorrow, if you can."

"I'll do my best."

Stephen walked back from Mr. Brown's office to the coach house at the rear of the high school, where Clarence had Cherokee hitched to the buggy, and ready to go.

"Thank you, Clarence. I'll see you in the morning."

"Good afternoon, Professor Harris. Say hello to Mrs. Harris for me."

"I'll do it. You take care, now."

He stepped up onto the front seat of the buggy, and took the reins in his hands. He flicked them once and clucked to Cherokee, and the bay gelding turned and made his way out to the pike, through the streets of Carnesville.

Stephen saw a couple of Model T Ford automobiles in town, and also spied an Oldsmobile. If the war had not popped up into his immediate future, he would have saved up his money and bought a Ford Model T himself.

Henry Ford's mass production techniques were making automobiles more affordable each year.

Cherokee began to trot over the dirt streets, until his shod hoofs hit the paved pike out of town. Stephen's thoughts were drawn to his weekend, and he remembered that he had only a few dry flies for his fly rod. He needed turkey feathers to tie more flies. He would go turkey hunting instead, and kill himself a turkey on Saturday.

He could then spend a little time during the week with some fresh yarn, and tie himself a decent number of dry flies from the turkey breast feathers.

He later drove the buggy down past Miss Irene's schoolhouse, where Annie and Millie were waiting out in the school yard. He waived to Miss Irene as he helped his girls into the front seat of the buggy. As Cherokee eased off, Annie stared up at him with her green eyes, and asked him a question.

15

"What did you teach 'em in class today, Pa?"

Stephen smiled, and then answered his daughter. "I outlined the War of 1812 and its causes for my American History class, and the Napoleonic War for my World History class."

Cherokee drove them down into a creek bottom, and across a small wooden bridge. Millie saw some trees across the creek that she had not noticed before.

"What kind of tree is that, Pa. The one with the leaves with the silver bottoms?"

Stephen looked over at the creek, as he flipped his reins forward. "That's a Bay tree, darling. It's not the same tree as one that gives us the Bay leaf for spices, though. It is a relative of the Magnolia."

They rode up an embankment, and Annie looked over and spied a blooming tree up the creek bed, which she pointed out to her father. "What's the pretty pink tree over there, Pa?"

Stephen looked further up the rocky creek bed, and saw a small tree that was covered with beautiful pink blossoms. It was colored a delicate pink, and its pink beauty stood out in the new leaves of the early spring forest along the creek bed.

"That is a Honeysuckle Tree my dear. It's even prettier than the Dogwoods, I think."

The Dogwood trees along the creek bottom were also in full bloom, and the trees looked like white clusters through the creek bottom and the tall slope of the hills beyond.

Cherokee continued his steady trot up Black Snake Road, until they began to near their large farm house. He then pricked up his ears, knowing that he was close to home, and his pace quickened.

He was a powerful animal, and he had worked up a good lather around his hind quarters pulling the buggy over the hills.

They soon rounded a bend in the road, where their white frame house could be seen across from a huge Black Oak Tree. The house was built in 1876 by Stephen's grandpa, David Harris, who had returned to North Georgia from an eleven year stay in Alabama.

David Harris had served as a sergeant in the First Alabama Union Cavalry during the Civil War, and lived over in Huntsville for a period of years after the war.

He bought the one hundred acre tract in 1876, and built a large barn and the house, and started a dairy.

The house was a beautiful two story building, with a wrap around front porch, and clapboards of Loblolly Pine. Stephen had the house painted white, and black shutters adorned each of the windows.

Loralie had put flower boxes on the front porch, and tulips were beginning to bloom on the top of their green stalks.

Stephen pulled the buggy around to the coach house beside the barn. The girls dismounted, and ran through the back door of the house to the kitchen. Loralie was in the process of cooking their supper.

Stephen smelled an aroma of peas and ham cooking on the wood stove in the kitchen as he led Cherokee into the barn.

He rubbed him down, carefully rubbing the muscles of the animal down on each leg. He hung up the harness and bit and bridle in the stalls of the barn, and led Cherokee into his stall. He gave him some hay and oats, and he took his water bucket out to the well pump off the back porch, and pumped it full of water. He watered Cherokee's water trough, and then walked into the kitchen.

Loralie was busy frying ham slices in a cast iron skillet. Stephen saw her eyes light up when he entered the room.

The girls had been put to work stacking wood from the wood pile outside of the house, to the wood box inside of the kitchen. Stephen hung up his coat in the hall closet, and came around the stove to greet Loralie.

She was busy frying ham slices on the stove, wearing a gray dress and a full white apron. Her honey blonde hair was pinned back in a bun, and Stephen thought she looked like a queen. He came up behind her, and wrapped his left arm around her waist. He nuzzled her right ear with his lips, and whispered softly to her. "Hello, beautiful. I missed you. You're always a sight to come home to."

She loved it when he nuzzled her, and she had missed him, too. It was kind of lonely when Stephen and the girls were gone all day.

She turned the ham pieces over in the skillet, put her fork down on a plate on the counter, and turned to face her tall husband.

"Let me greet you properly, sir." She then put her arms around him, and kissed Stephen full on the mouth.

The girls walked into the room, and witnessed their parents kissing one another.

They blushed and smiled at each other, but they were both happy that their parents truly loved each other. They had friends from other homes that were not nearly as happy as theirs.

Stephen saw the girls in between kisses, and told them to wash up and set the table for their mother. He kissed Loralie another time and patted her behind when he saw the girls weren't looking their way.

He walked out to the spring house, and poured some new milk from a big milk can into a pewter pitcher.

He took out his pocket knife, and cut a small piece of cheese off of the big round of cheese on a stone shelf near the floor. He put the cheese on a plate he had brought with him, and he walked back around the barn and into the kitchen.

He handed the pitcher to Loralie, who began to fill the girl's glasses with milk. The table was set with their second best china, and two large bowls on the table contained steaming black eyed peas and potatoes. A plate of corn bread sat next to a plate of fried ham. Stephen watched Loralie walk over to the oven, and carefully pull out a deep dish pear pie.

Loralie had canned a number of Keifer Pears from their tree that fall, and now she had baked a pie with one of their last jars of pears.

Stephen's mouth watered, as Loralie brought the deep dish pie over to the table.

"Sit down children, and I will return thanks."

Millie and Annie took their seats, while Stephen poured coffee for Loralie and himself. He helped Loralie into her chair, and then took his seat at the head of the table. They all held hands and bowed their heads, and Stephen began to ask the blessing.

"Lord, we thank you for this food, and for all of our many blessings. Let us ever be mindful of the needs of others. Bless this food to the nourishment of our bodies, we ask in Jesus' name,

Amen."

The table sprang to life after the blessing, as busy hands all around began to heap all of their plates with food.

Loralie had fried some corn bread that night in two hoe cakes, and their aroma caught Stephen's nostrils. He liked hoe cakes every now and then, but he preferred his corn bread baked in the oven.

They began to eat the delicious meal that Loralie had prepared, and the topic of conversation around the table centered on the varsity baseball game scheduled for the next day.

Loralie asked Stephen about the new uniforms.

"They came in today. I will give them out after the first period of class tomorrow."

"Who paid for all these new uniforms?"

"Ty Cobb sent the money down from Detroit. He sent me a telegram a couple of months ago and offered to buy the team brand new uniforms. I took him up on it. I sent him a telegram back to his hotel in Vero Beach when the Tigers were in spring training down there."

Ty Cobb was a native of Royston. His father had been a history professor at Franklin County High School years before. Stephen was his favorite student. Professor Cobb was shot and killed by his wife, who had supposedly mistaken him for a burglar. Most people believed that the wife's lover shot the Professor to death.

Ty Cobb went on to fame and stardom as a Detroit Tigers outfielder, and he was the pride of Royston, Georgia.

The girls were excited about the fact that their father had corresponded with the great Major League ballplayer.

"Pa, why would Ty Cobb send you money to buy a high school team uniforms?"

Stephen swallowed a slice of ham, and washed it down with his creamed coffee.

"Because, Millie, he has never forgotten his home town, even though he has achieved stardom and success. He never forgot his roots."

He looked over at Loralie, remembering his duties as baseball coach. "Did you pack my cleats and glove in my canvas bag for tomorrow?"

Loralie sipped on her coffee, and cooly answered him. "Yes, dear, it is packed and sitting at the back of the hall closet. Have a piece of pie, dear."

She handed him a desert plate filled with steaming deep dish pear pie. Stephen spooned it into his mouth, and then promptly downed the whole dish of pie.

"That pie was a masterpiece, my dear."

They soon finished their meal. Stephen asked the girls to start cleaning the table and washing the dishes, as he wanted to talk to their mother for a few minutes on the front porch.

He took Loralie by the hand, and led her around to the swing on the front porch. The sun was setting over the rim of a large hill the locals described as Buzzard Knob, and its orange brilliance lit up the western sky.

Loralie commented on the sunset.

"It's really beautiful tonight." She sat down on the wooden swing, and Stephen sat beside her.

"So are you, my love." Stephen put his arm around Loralie, and kissed her tenderly on her lips. His lips sought hers, and he kissed her deeply.

"There is something that I must tell you, darling. I went to the Sheriff and asked him to help me obtain a commission in a National Guard regiment. If I get drafted into the Army, I want to be an officer."

Loralie drew away from him, Her green eyes infused with anger at the thought of what Stephen had done.

"Have you forgotten that we have two daughters to raise?"

"No, but we are now at war with Germany. I want our daughters to be able to safely travel on ocean liners without fear of U-Boats."

"What kind of problem is that in Royston, Georgia? We have no ocean here."

"It is all our problem. I'm going to be drafted anyway. You should know that. I would rather be an officer leading men, since that is really what I do now. I owe the Germans something anyhow."

"Stephen, no matter what you do, you will not be able to bring your father back. He died in Cuba, and nothing you do can change that."

"I know, but I can lead men, and make a difference in a local volunteer regiment. I have asked the governor to grant me a commission as a lieutenant in an infantry regiment."

Loralie knew that it was useless to argue. Stephen was going to war. It would be better if he were an officer, where his leadership skills could count.

"I can't stand the thought of you being gone away to France. Please hold me, dear. Let us just enjoy the moment while we can."

He held her tight against him while they watched the sun set over Buzzard Knob.

CHAPTER TWO

The next day, Stephen and some other teachers handed out the new baseball uniforms to the team after first period class.

That same day, Stephen taught both of his history classes, and took his lunch bucket with him up the street to George Mason's drug store. He bought several crackers from the cracker barrel, and sat down at the soda fountain.

A nineteen year old sandy haired young man, Sam Turner, was the soda jerk. He was dressed in blue jeans and a white apron, and wore a white bifold cap. Stephen ordered a Coca Cola, as he loved the taste of the new soft drink.

He also thought the carbonated water in the soda settled his stomach, as he always got a nervous stomach before his varsity games.

The soda jerk poured the Coca Cola syrup from a pump at the fountain into a marked glass up to the fill line above the bottom. He then set the glass under the soda fountain, and poured carbonated water into the glass. He then took a narrow spoon and stirred the soda, and placed ice cubes into the glass.

Stephen handed him twenty cents for the soda and the crackers. He then took out his pocket knife, and his cheese that he had cut the night before, which he had wrapped in cheesecloth in his lunch bucket.

He cut the cheese into strips, and began to eat the cheese and crackers, and to drink his Coca Cola. He thought about the baseball game against the Commerce Royals, and about his pitching match ups with the Commerce players. Most of the locals shied away from him during his pre-game meal at the drug store, as they thought it would bring bad luck to the team.

Stephen ate his crackers and cheese, drank his Coca Cola, and then thanked Sam Turner the soda jerk. He walked out of the drug store, up the street to the high school, and down to locker room. The team was already dressed, and the players were heading out to the baseball diamond.

He walked to his locker, removed his clothing, and put on his baseball uniform. He pulled on his sanitary socks and stockings, and pulled on his baseball spikes. He got his fungo bat, a regular wooden bat, his lineup card and a pencil, and headed out onto the field.

As he walked through the locker room, he looked at himself in the mirror. A lion paw was embroidered across his jersey, along with the word "LIONS" in bold green letters. A white "F" adorned the cap, with a lion paw patch showing on the left side of the cap.

Stephen was leading his team into battle, and there was nothing like a varsity baseball game to get his blood pumping.

The Franklin County Lions won the baseball game in the bottom of the ninth inning on a squeeze play with one out. Scott Beck, the second baseman, laid down a perfect squeeze bunt on the third base line. The bunt allowed Willie Carter to dash in with the winning run from third base.

The team had won ten games and lost none up to that point in the season. Stephen addressed the team after the game in the locker room, congratulating them on a job well done. He changed into his street clothes in the locker room, drank a little water, and went to the coach house for his horse and buggy. Loralie and the girls met him there.

Loralie was lovely, as she had on a yellow dress and a straw hat with a blue ribbon. Ned Sanders was with them, and had brought them over in his wagon. Annie and Millie were in their school clothes, blue dresses with matching dark shoes. They had their lunch pails dangling from their right hands.

Loralie congratulated Stephen with a full kiss on his lips. He put his arm around her waist, and began to whisper into her ear. "Why don't you have the girls ride back home with Ned, and you come along with me. I have a surprise for you."

Loralie's eyes lit up, and she began to ask Stephen about the surprise, but then thought otherwise. She told the girls to ride back home with Ned, and then walked back to Stephen's buggy. She climbed up into the buggy at the coach house, as Clarence held Cherokee by his harness.

Cherokee was chomping at the bit, anxious to pull off and hit the road, but Stephen held him back. He wanted Ned's horse to get a good start on them, because he wanted to be alone with Loralie. After he waited a few minutes, he clucked to Cherokee, and he began to pull the buggy at a trot down the streets of Carnesville. Loralie was curious, as this was unusual behavior from her husband on a Thursday afternoon.

"What are you doing Steve? You sure are acting funny."

Stephen looked over at her, and could not help but admire her beauty. "I have a surprise for you, honey, and I just wanted to be alone with you when you first see it."

Loralie's green eyes twinkled, as she held onto the back of her straw hat. "That really tells me a lot, dear. This could be anything."

Stephen flipped the reins out onto Cherokee's rump. "Just trust me. The wait will be worth it, I believe."

Cherokee trotted down the pike out of town, and soon began to pull the buggy back toward Black Snake Road. Near Buzzard Knob, Stephen turned off the main road, and Cherokee began to pull the buggy up a dirt road that led toward the top of a high hill.

Two thirds of the way up, Stephen turned off onto a drive in front of the remains of the Brady place. The Brady house was destroyed by fire twenty years before, and Ma Brady moved into town rather than rebuild the structure. Only the chimney and foundation stones remained. Out in the yard, a large Black Oak tree dominated the scenery, with a wide trunk that was fifty inches wide at the stump. Its branches towered above the old home place, appearing that time of year as huge outstretching arms for visitors. Stephen reined in Cherokee under the Black Oak tree.

"Ok, here is the surprise. Our anniversary is at the end of the month, but I went to the jeweler and ordered you a gift two weeks ago. It came in today. Here it is."

He produced a small box from his gray waistcoat pocket, wrapped in a white ribbon. Loralie removed her straw hat, and took the box from her husband. She untied the ribbon, and opened the box slowly. It contained a white gold locket, in the shape of a heart, with a blue Sapphire in the center. Loralie's eyes lit up when she saw it. "Oh, darling, I love it! It is so beautiful. Please put it on for me."

Stephen unclasped the locket, and put it around Loralie's neck. "The blue Sapphire is a special color, darling. Blue stands for devotion and duty and faithfulness. It is a symbol of my never ending love and devotion to you, darling. I know you got angry at me for writing and requesting a commission. I hope you can forgive me, and remember how much I really love you."

His hand went to her breast, as his lips sought hers at once. He began to whisper to her. "I told Millie to start supper without us, that we would be along in a little while."

He reached around the seat of the buggy and pulled a folded quilt from his equipment bag. He got down and walked over to a grassy knoll, where he spread the quilt on the ground. He then walked around the buggy and picked Loralie up effortlessly, and carried her over to the quilt. "Sometimes, love, just telling you that I love you is not enough. Right now, I need to show you."

Loralie reached out for him. "Come down and kiss me, Professor. You talk too much."

Stephen began to kiss Loralie, and then proceeded to make love to her under the huge branches of the Black Oak tree.

Early the next Saturday morning, Stephen arose at four a.m., and milked the cow. He was dressed in his olive khaki shirt and trousers, together with his high top hunting boots. He milked the cow quickly, and sat the milk pail in the spring house, where he covered it with cheesecloth.

He cut himself a piece of cheese, and wrapped the cheese in a piece of wax paper that he carried in his haversack. He had a piece of bread cut to go with the cheese, which would serve as his dinner later on that day.

He filled his tin canteen at the outdoor well pump, and he went to the storeroom after his rifle. He kept the ammunition for the .30-.40

caliber bolt action rifle on a shelf above the gun. He found two clips of ammunition by feeling around in the darkness of the storeroom. The rifle had belonged to William Harris when he had served with the Rough Riders in Cuba. Ned Sanders had smuggled the rifle out past U.S. Army quartermasters and into the United States after William was killed on the San Juan Heights.

Stephen wanted to use the rifle on the turkey hunt in order to get used to shooting the bolt action rifle. The U. S. Army would issue him an Enfield or a Springfield rifle to use in the coming war.

He grabbed his turkey box call, his pigskin brim hat, and a green feed sack, and he set out on his turkey hunt.

The moon shone out over his left shoulder, in its quarter phase, as he began his hike up the knob, with his Krag-Jorgenson rifle slung over his shoulder with a cotton sling. He could see the mist rising off of the hardwood trees on the ridge, as he began his ascent up the small mountain on a narrow deer path.

He heard a couple of birds flutter over to different tree limbs in the trees around him. He stopped a few minutes later when he thought he heard the distant cry of a mountain panther across the knob.

His destination was a small stream that sprang up about two thirds of the way up the mountain. Turkeys often roosted near water, and there were giant White Oak trees nearby that provided good roosting spots. He saw the yellow outline of the eastern horizon, and noticed that dawn would break in less than an hour.

He closed to within two hundred and fifty yards of the spring, and stepped into the woods off of the deer trail. He decided to locate a gobbler with the use of a locator call. He began to hoot and imitate the call of a male Barred Owl. He called loudly, but uniformly, and with a mechanical tone that was similar to the call of a real Barred Owl.

One hundred and fifty yards to his left, over in some White Oak trees, the call was answered by a gobble from a tom turkey on the roost. Stephen's heart began to pound. He had located his prey! He carefully and quietly began to ease over to the left, in the general direction of where he had heard the gobbler.

He stepped carefully and quietly, cutting the distance between him and the gobbler, without getting too close to the wary tom turkey. He spied a small meadow just beyond the stream, about seventy five yards from the tree where he believed the tom turkey was roosting.

He selected an uprooted Loblolly Pine tree as his set up point, as it offered him concealment, but also a view of the meadow below. He noticed that the eastern sky had turned a bright pink, as the sun would be rising shortly.

He took a seat behind the roots of the blown down pine, noticing that the old tree was really huge near its base. He pulled his green feed sack from his haversack, removed his hat, and pulled the sack over his head. He pulled the cut eye holes around where he could see, and fumbled around in his haversack again.

He carefully pulled out his box call, along with a piece of chalk. He began to chalk the sides of the box call, which was made of Eastern Red Cedar. Ned Sanders made the call for him over twelve years before. When he was satisfied that the call was chalked, he set it down on a mossy rock near his right hip.

He took the rifle off of his shoulder, and pulled a clip from his haversack. The clip contained six rounds. He checked to make sure that the safety was on, and he fed the clip into the magazine of the rifle. He pulled the bolt back, however, and fed the clip down while pulling the bolt back into position. By holding the clip down while the bolt was passing over, he had the magazine loaded, but did not have a round in the chamber. He would chamber a round only upon the approach of the turkey.

After he completed his preparations, he noticed that daylight was rapidly approaching, as the dawn was breaking. He saw Wrens and Cardinals flutter through the trees around him. He saw Gray Squirrels and Fox Squirrels crawling down on the trees around him. He then heard turkeys flying down from the oak trees near the spring above him.

After a few minutes, he took the cedar box call, and began to move the paddle of the call across the sides of the box, producing the yelping sounds of a turkey hen. Another hen answered him from seventy yards away. He then heard the thunderous gobble of a mature tom turkey around sixty yards away. In the morning mist, even though he had heard it many times before, the sound of the gobbler always sounded explosive. It was enough to stop Stephen's heart.

He began to make more yelping sounds on the box call. The gobbler gobbled twice more. This time it sounded closer. He was moving down the knob, apparently in Stephen's direction.

Stephen waited three minutes, then hit the box call again for a couple of yelps. This time the turkey triple gobbled. He was now twenty yards closer.

Stephen peered over the top of the tree trunk, and spied three black shapes coming in his direction. The daylight was increasing, and the approaching shapes began to take form. He saw a huge gobbler approaching with two turkey hens. He chambered a round into the Krag-Jorgenson carbine. He slowly brought the gun barrel across his chest, and into a position where he could take aim. He propped the gun barrel across a tree root, and took up the box call one last time.

He yelped two small yelps on the box call. The gobbler gobbled again, and kept coming. Stephen put the box call down, and took up his rifle. His heart was beating fast, but his experience in those situations took control.

When the tom turkey gobbled again, he stretched his neck out. At fifty yards with a rifle, it was a difficult shot at best. The hens with the gobbler were also coming his way. If they saw him or got suspicious, they would putt, and sound the alarm to the rest of the flock, and the game would be over.

Stephen's luck soon changed, however. The gobbler went into a strut at fifty yards from his position. Stephen clicked the safety off, and aimed the sights of the carbine just over the red markings at the base of the gobbler's neck.

The gobbler's tail was in the shape of a fan, with the white tips of the tail feathers showing. His wings were stretched out to the sides, and he was in the process of gobbling when Stephen squeezed the trigger and fired. The rifle recoiled against his shoulder, and Stephen saw the tom turkey crumple and hit the ground.

The hens turned and putted twice, and then ran off when Stephen removed his mask and stood up. He clicked his rifle over to "safety," and then walked over to where the gobbler fell.

He reached over and examined the spurs on the bird. They were over two inches long. He had a long beard as well. The gobbler was at least three years old. Stephen lifted the bird by his feet, and estimated his weight at over twenty pounds. The rifle round had almost severed the turkey's neck.

Stephen grabbed his canteen and took a long drink of water. He took out his clasp knife and cut himself a piece of cheese and a slice of bread, and began to eat his lunch standing up. He reached into his pocket and pulled out his railroad watch. It was only 7:45 a.m. He pulled the dead bird over his shoulder, and began the long hike down the knob, and home to his family. He would have baked turkey and dressing tomorrow, and turkey soup tonight from the wings and the leg meat.

CHAPTER THREE

During the middle of June, Stephen and Annie rode down with Ned Sanders to deliver a load of milk and cheese to the depot at Royston. Ned drove a team of grey mules, pulling a wagon load of milk cans and boxed cheese bound up in Basswood hoops.

The day was warm, and Stephen noticed the pretty ribbons Loralie had tied in Annie's hair that morning. Annie's facial features resembled her father, but her sky blue eyes and her blond hair were similar to her mother's. However, her hair grew out of her scalp the same way as Stephen's hair. He looked over at his pretty daughter, as she pointed out animals on the side of the road.

They spotted Cottontail rabbits and several different birds on their way out Black Snake Road and into town. Ned had planted wheat early that spring, and began making serious money selling cheese to the War Department.

Stephen had a few dollars in his pocket, and promised Annie that he would get her an ice cream soda from the drug store in town. He decided to indulge himself with a milk shake once he and Ned made their delivery. They arrived in town forty five minutes later, and the lathered mules pulled them around to the depot. They unloaded their wagon an hour later, and collected Ned's weigh bill from the railroad clerk. They then drove up the street to Arnold's drug store.

Stephen dropped Annie off there, and he pushed twenty cents into the front pocket of her overalls before they shoved off again. She would get Millie a lolly pop from Arnold's store after she was done at the soda fountain.

Ned had promised Loralie that he would help Stephen bring home some fresh fruits and vegetables from the farmer's market. At the market, Stephen was looking at some fresh peaches, when he was hailed by twelve year old Jeff Pender, who was employed at the *Western Union* office. He tipped the leather bill of his cap to Stephen, and handed him a telegram.

"Mr. Ned told me that I could find you here, Professor Harris."

"Thank you, Jeffrey. Here is a nickel. Go buy yourself some ice cream when you end your shift today."

The boy's eyes lit up. "Oh, thank you, sir. I sure will." He pocketed the nickel, and trotted up the street. Stephen put down his basket of peaches, and opened the envelope containing the telegram:

Western Union
June 15, 1917

To: First Lt. Stephen Harris, Georgia National Guard
From: Russell Elliott, Counsel to Gov. Wm. Slayton

GOVERNOR SLAYTON HAS APPOINTED YOU AS A FIRST LT. IN COMPANY "G" 25th GA GUARD REGIMENT STOP. ORDERS AND YOUR COMMISSION SHALL BE FORTHCOMING FROM ADJUTANT GENERAL'S OFFICE STOP. THIS APPOINTMENT IS CONDITIONED ON YOUR COMPLETION OF OFFICER'S CANDIDATE SCHOOL AT CAMP GORDON NEXT MONTH STOP. ORDERS SHALL ALSO ISSUE BY U.S. MAIL THIS MONDAY AM.

BY ORDER OF GOV. WM. SLAYTON

Stephen read the telegram, and realized that he was about to enter the U.S. Army. President Wilson had begun the process of nationalizing all of the state National Guard units into the U.S. Army. Stephen's regiment would certainly become part of the mobilized army in the near future.

He was excited about his commission, but he also realized that his assignment would cause him to leave home before the end of the summer.

He then also realized that he would have only a short period of time to spend with his family that summer. He hurriedly bought some pink eyed peas at the market, along with a half bushel of South Carolina peaches. He found Ned up the street, and asked him if he could go with him to the Atlantic Ice Company.

They drove down to the ice company, where Stephen purchased a fifty pound block of ice packed in sawdust. They drove the wagon back to Arnold's drug store, where Stephen located Annie. He told her that he had a surprise for all of them. She did not understand when Stephen bought rock salt and a funny looking churn at the store, but Ned's eyes lit up with recognition when he carried the stuff out to the wagon.

"Why Annie, we-uns is gonna make ice cream when we get home. What flavor are we gonna have, Steve?"

Stephen winked at Ned. "Once you get some of the peaches cut up and peeled, I reckon it will be peach."

He had gone to a lot of expense to make this treat for Ned and his family, but he would be gone soon, and he wanted to make this special treat for his family before he left for the war.

They drove home quickly. Stephen quickly milked the cow, while Ned peeled and cut up the peaches. Loralie was soon let in on their scheme, and she cooked the milk on the stove for a short while, while adding eggs, peaches, and sugar to the concoction. She then poured the mixture into the metal can of the churn, and brought it around to the front porch. Ned got the ax, and carefully chipped away chunks of ice, and then carefully placed the ice around the metal pan, and between the wooden walls of the churn. Stephen added the rock salt to the ice, and installed the hand crank on the top of the churn. The girls then took turns with Ned cranking the churn.

They occasionally added more chipped ice and rock salt, and an hour later, their efforts were rewarded with frozen peach ice cream. Ned saddled up Cherokee, and rode over to his place to get Carl. They both returned thirty minutes later, and joined the Harris family while they were eating up all of the delicious ice cream. They had to eat it all, because they had no electric freezer or icebox to store their finished product in.

When the ice cream was devoured, Loralie walked up to Stephen, and placed her arms around his neck. "Why did you buy the ice and the churn today?"

"Well, I thought about treating myself and Annie to an ice cream soda, and then I thought I could spend a little more money and treat all of us to a bowl of ice cream. That block of ice is so large, we can have iced tea for dinner tomorrow, and churn a different flavor of ice cream for dessert."

Loralie kissed him on the lips. "I never know what to expect from you, dear."

Stephen did not have the heart to tell Loralie about his telegram. He would tell her another day. This day belonged to his family. His girls were having a ball. Ice cream at home! They held hands on the front porch, and watched Annie and Millie and Carl playing tag out in the front yard.

Ned had grabbed a pan, and began shelling the peas they had bought in town. Their big yellow cur, Rex, was under the edge of the porch, licking up some ice cream Annie had spilled there. It was a wonderful Summer afternoon, Stephen thought. His thoughts then focused on Europe, and the World War that was raging over in France. How much longer did he have with his family here in America, before he would go off to the war?

The following morning, Stephen walked over to Ned Sanders' dairy to speak to Ned, who was in the process of raking hay.

Ned stopped his mule rake, and wiped sweat from his brow. Stephen offered him a drink from his canteen. Stephen wasted little time.

"Ned, I got a telegram from the Governor's chief counsel yesterday. I'll have a first lieutenant's commission next week. I have to go to the officers' candidate school at Camp Gordon though."

"How is your family gonna get by when you go off to fight the war?" Ned took another swallow of spring water from Stephens's canteen.

"I'll have the army start an allotment from my pay, and have most of my pay sent home. I spoke to Robert Miller two weeks ago, and I am going to pay him to do work around my place after I am gone."

Ned pulled his reins tighter, to hold up his mule. "I expect Carl to be drafted, though, since he is twenty one years old. He is a great shot, Steve. He'll make a fine soldier."

Stephen scratched the back of his head and began to nervously address Ned about the subject of his son.

"Ned, I believe Carl would make a good first sergeant. He's bright, he knows how to handle a gun, and he does what he is told to do. He would stand a better chance of surviving the war if he went through the extra training for an NCO at Camp Gordon."

Ned reached for his handkerchief, and wiped more sweat from his forehead. "Steve, you're right. I guess I can ask Claude Cook if he can send his boy Russell over to help me, once Carl goes off to serve. You know Steve, life moves in circles, I believe."

"Why is that?"

"Well, in '98, I was your father's first sergeant in Cuba, and now in 1917, you want Carl to be your First Sergeant. What comes around goes around, the way I see it."

"Well, I never thought about it that way, Ned, but you're right. I should know by next week when we have to report to Camp Gordon."

"I'll speak to Claude tomorrow, Steve. You need to tell Loralie tonight, though. Why don't you take her over to Carnesville for dinner tonight. I'll watch the girls for you. Maybe your news will go down easier if she hears it while you are eating a fine dinner at the hotel. You gotta break this sort of news easy to her, son. Women can't stand this kind of stuff, and with good reason. There are a hell of a lot of widows in England right now. Europe has turned into a killing machine. You have a tough sale to make on Loralie. Good luck."

"Thank you, Ned. Daddy always told me to listen to your advice. I'll bring the girls over by five o'clock."

"We'll see you then."

True to his word, Stephen asked Loralie to dress up that evening, as he had plans to take her to dinner at the Butler House Inn in that evening.

They dropped the children off with Ned at 5:30, and Stephen drove the buggy over the pike into Carnesville.

They had a romantic dinner at a table near the double window, which had a view of the lovely daylilies in the garden nearby. Stephen took Loralie's hand, and broke the news to her. She began to tremble and then began asking questions of Stephen.

"How will you support us, if you are gone off to war?"

"I'll have 90 percent of my officer's pay sent home to you and the girls, to the account we have at the Merchant's Bank here in town."

"Is Carl going to go into the service, too?"

"Yeah, he is going to go to Officers' Candidate School, but he will be a sergeant."

"How is Ned going to run his dairy without him?"

"Russell Cook, Claude's boy, says he can hire out at the dairy for a fair wage while Carl is gone. Carl is going to send a good portion of his pay home to his Pa, you know, to help him out.

"Well, I see you have everything all figured out." Loralie then took Stephen's hand. "Have you figured out what we are to do if you don't come back?"

Stephen knew that question was coming. "I have purchased three life insurance policies with the Metropolitan Life Insurance Company through our agent in Athens. The original policies are in my safety deposit box over at the Merchant's Bank. If I should be killed in action, you will need to contact Kenneth Smith over at the bank, get the original policies, and file a death claim with the company."

"I wasn't just talking about money, Stephen, and you know it. What are the girls going to do without their father? What would I do without my husband?" Tears began to well up in Loralie's green eyes.

Stephen began to feel uncomfortable in the hotel dining room. He waived over a waiter and ordered them both a cup of coffee. He then took Loralie by her hand, looked into her eyes, and spoke slowly to her. "Darling, if I am killed, you and the girls would suffer, I'm sure.

But you would do your best to survive without me. The girls are growing into young women. I know that they would make both of us proud of them as they get older."

"What about me, Stephen? What about those long, lonely nights when I will have nothing to do but lay there and wonder if you are dead or alive? How can I ever get through the loneliness of being parted from you for months and years? When will this mad war ever end? The newspaper reports all the killing in France, and it all just seems for nothing."

Stephen knew that their debate had to be brought to closure. "Darling, Congress has declared war. The Selective Service System has started drafting young men from our county into the service. My number would have been pulled at any time. As an officer, I *can make a difference*. As a private, I would stand an almost equal chance of being killed, and my leadership abilities would be wasted. If we do what our President asks of all of us, we will win this war, and then come home. I know that it is going to be a dirty, lousy, cruel job, but sometimes that is what must be done.

"I don't expect you to understand all of the issues and reasons that led us to war, but I hope and pray that you will be here for me when I get back. I have always loved you, and I only want to spend the rest of my days with you. Please don't be angry at me for serving my country, darling."

Loralie's eyes softened a little, and then she had another question. "When do you report to Officers' Candidate School?"

"In two weeks. We report to Camp John B. Gordon. We will do six weeks of Officer Candidate Training, and then they will send us out into the field with the enlisted men.

Stephen and Loralie finished their dinner on a sour note, after they both realized that neither one could dissuade the other about the war. As they drove home, Loralie asked him to hold her close, as she wanted to feel his body next to hers. If he was joining the army in two weeks, she wanted to claim him for as long as she could.

CHAPTER FOUR

In July, 1917, Stephen and Carl Sanders were ordered to report to Camp John B. Gordon, near Norcross, Georgia. Stephen asked Ned to drive them to the train depot in his wagon. He had said his goodbyes to Loralie and the girls, and he promised to write them often.

At the depot in Royston, they took their small suitcases and boarded a steam train for the short ride to Elberton. When they arrived in Elberton, they transferred to another train at the Elberton station, and began to ride on the line west through Madison County, and the town of Comer. After passing the station, Stephen broke out their lunches that Loralie had packed for them in a shoe box.

They dined on chicken salad sandwiches, pickles, deviled eggs, and washed their meal down with lemonade from Stephen's canteen.

The train took on wood and water in Athens, along with more soldiers. One of the new passengers was Richard Mabry, a county commissioner from Madison County. He had substantial political connections in Atlanta, and managed to land a captain's commission. After the train took on water, wood, and passengers, it pulled out of the station, across the middle Oconee river, and over toward Winder. Stephen pulled his campaign hat over his eyes, and took a short nap, as the train made its way through Auburn, and made a scheduled stop in Lawrenceville.

The train then steamed out of Lawrenceville and through Lilburn. At Rockbridge Station, the train was halted and all of the officer candidates were instructed to leave the train with their baggage.

They were met on the other side of the train station by a six foot sergeant major named Frank Pendergrass. Sergeant Major Pendergrass instructed each of the men to load their baggage onto a large GMC truck at the end of the depot, and to line up on the other side of the railroad tracks facing north.

They were then told to march, and they marched along the Rockbridge Road six miles or so to the sleepy little mill village of

Norcross. They marched another mile above Norcross to Camp John B. Gordon, a camp composed of wooden buildings with tin roofs. Carpenters could be seen erecting similar buildings on the other end of the camp.

The sergeant major then ordered the men to divide into two groups, one for NCO's, and the other for commissioned officers. They were then ordered to stand at attention, as a tall six foot two inch officer with eagles on his shoulder straps walked out to address them. He wore a campaign hat, and was dressed in an olive green army uniform. The neck of his uniform carried a crossed rifle insignia, with "U.S." in brass in the middle. He began to speak.

"Men, I am Colonel Charles Harker. I have been ordered to take command of the 325th Infantry regiment, which was formerly the 25th Georgia National Guard Regiment. You will become the officers and NCOs of that regiment. Six weeks from now, your men will arrive here as draftees, and it will be your job to train them for combat.

"Now, it will be our job to train you for combat, so you can train your men when they arrive here. First, though, you will report to the Quartermaster for your uniforms, and then you will secure your gear in your footlockers in your barracks. Later this afternoon, Major Charles Witherspoon of the Canadian Army will begin your instruction.

"This camp is named after General John B. Gordon, who at one time commanded one of the most effective brigades in the Confederate Army. When we complete your training, you will be one of the best trained regiments in Uncle Sam's Army. Fall in behind Sergeant Major Pendergrass, now, and you will be issued you uniforms. That is all."

Stephen got in line behind Richard Maby, and they marched over to the Quartermasters. In single file, they received four pairs of olive green socks, puttees, a rain poncho, a blanket, a knapsack, one pair of 1917 Trench Boots, a haversack, and a campaign hat.

They were then directed to their barracks, where Sgt. Major Pendergrass instructed them as to the proper method for storing their clothing and gear in their footlockers. After a quick trip to the mess hall, the men were instructed to march out to a small field at the rear of B barracks, and to sit in a semicircle.

A few minutes later, a one armed man wearing a major's uniform of the Canadian Army walked up, and began to address them. His left arm had been amputated above the elbow, and the sleeve was pinned to his uniform tunic.

He wore an officer's dress cap, but displayed an air of confidence as he addressed them.

"Men, I am Major Charles Witherspoon of the Canadian Army. Your War Department has asked me to help train you men over the next six weeks, to make officers out of you. In the morning, you will begin to learn the basics of marching in formation and drilling, and you will learn Army regulations in the afternoon.

"I want to discuss the big picture today, and give you an overview on the War. Right now, Britain and France are getting the bad end of it from the Huns. It is going to be up to you and your men to win this war. It will be your job to kill enough German soldiers and to recapture enough territory to compel the Kaiser to sue for peace. Your work will not be easy, though.

"Your grandfathers fought for the Confederacy and struggled and died just a few miles or so below here. The battlefields that you will fight on in France will be much deadlier, though. We now have high explosive shells; our artillery has better range, and is much more accurate. A German shell took my arm at Ypres. They now fire poison gas shells that produce poison clouds of death in a few minutes.

"Aeroplanes can fly over your trenches and drop bombs on you, and shoot you up with their machine guns. The Krauts put up barbed wire to slow you down, and then they shoot you up with the rapid fire of their machine guns. The Germans also have heavy storm troopers that attack you with flame throwing equipment and burn you to death. If you get past all of the dangers on the battlefield, the average German soldier is trained to shoot you to death with his 7 mm Mauser rifle, or give you the bayonet.

41

"As you can see, winning this war will be a challenge for you and your men. I will train you well, though. I will teach you how to survive, and how to attack the Hun, and take the fight to him. Get some rest, and we will start at 0600 hours tomorrow. That is all for today."

The major walked back toward the headquarters hut, while Sgt. Major Pendergrass dismissed them. They were to clean and oil their boots, pack their civilian clothing to be sent home, and be ready to sack out at 0930 hours.

Camp Gordon, Georgia
July 17, 1917

Dearest Loralie:

I sit here before tattoo, and write you as quickly as I can, to let you know that things are fine here in camp. We have been going out marching in the mornings, around ten miles or so up toward Duluth, and then back again. We study the Army Regulations each day, and learn all of the drill commands for marching, and the complete manual of arms.

Next week, we will go out on the rifle range, located about eight miles from camp, and we will have target practice. How have you been? I have missed both you and the girls dearly. I miss you more than you will ever know. I miss you darling, and the wonderful life that we had together. The toughest part of being a soldier is being separated from those that you love.

Hopefully soon, we will draw a weekend pass, and I will hop a train up to Royston. Tell Ned that Carl is doing fine. Lori, I saw Ned post a letter to Sheila McRae yesterday. I didn't know that he was courting her!

I hear the bugler blowing tattoo now, love. I have to go now. I will see you soon.

Your loving husband,
Stephen

On Monday of the following week, Sgt. Major Pendergrass directed the Officer Candidates to the quartermaster's shed, where they were issued ammunition belts. The men were then directed to several GMC trucks near the edge of the camp. They climbed into the trucks, and the large vehicles were cranked and driven down the road toward the rifle range.

They arrived at the range a half hour later, where Major Witherspoon arrived to greet them at the main compound. He was holding a British Enfield .303 bolt action rifle.

"Men, this is an Enfield .303 caliber bolt action rifle. It is substantially similar to your Springfield Rifle, which is .30 caliber. The rifle fires a conical bullet from a brass smokeless cartridge. The cartridges come packed in brass clips, which you will load into the magazine of the weapon when you are ready to fire.

"The clips come to us packed in bandoliers. Each bandolier holds sixty cartridges, arranged in six pockets, each holding two clips. This rifle has a maximum range of over 4800 yards. Its muzzle velocity is 2800 feet per second.

"When it is time for you to fire at your target, your instructor will give you a clip of ammunition, and you will load your rifle. When he gives you the OK to fire, you will commence firing at the large target that is located two hundred and fifty yards down the rifle range. Let's see."

The major put the rifle down on a table, and pulled out his duty roster, which he had on a clipboard. "I need to select one candidate to show you the correct technique. Candidate Harris, please step forward."

Stephen walked forward, and accepted the weapon from Major Witherspoon. "Take the clip of ammunition, and proceed to the first firing position over there. You are to fire at the target over there from a standing position. The target is two hundred and fifty yards away. Here is your clip. Proceed to the firing area."

"Yes, sir." Stephen opened the bolt of the rifle and took the clip from the major. He then walked over to the firing line.

"Load the weapon, and fire at will at the bulls eye on the target, Mr. Harris. Fire one round."

"Yes, sir."

Stephen pushed the clip down into the magazine of the rifle. He pulled the bolt back, and pushed it forward, chambering a round from the magazine. He took the safety off the weapon, aimed at the bulls eye on the target, and fired.

The gun recoiled back. A team of fire control officers seated in the pits beneath the target cranked the target in front of the pit down. They yelled back down the gun range. "Bull's eye at ten o'clock." They marked the hit on the black bulls eye with a round piece of white tape, and then they cranked the target back up so the hit could be seen from the front of the firing range.

"Nice shooting, Mr. Harris. Chamber another round. Fire at will, but allow thirty seconds between your shots."

"Yes, sir."

Stephen chambered another round, took aim, and fired. The target was again cranked down, and the shot was marked. "Bull's eye. Dead center."

Stephen fired again. The target was again cranked down. "Bull's eye." He fired his remaining rounds, hitting the bull's eye each time. The fire control officers began to talk to one another. "Damn! This guy is really good!"

The major grabbed a bullhorn, and shouted down the range to the fire control officers. "Lieutenant Lester, bring me that target, if you will." After the target was brought up, he studied the holes for a few moments, and then looked up at Stephen. "Mister Harris, we will skip the rest of *your* rifle training for today. You will be rated above that of a sharpshooter. From what I see today, you will be rated as an 'expert' marksman on the company books. Come with me over to the pistol range, Mister Harris. Let's see what you can do with the Colt auto loading pistol."

Later that afternoon, Stephen was checked out with a Government Colt 1911 .45 caliber pistol. He fired the pistol at targets fifty yards away, from kneeling and standing positions. Stephen didn't tell the major that he had grown up shooting his father's .38 caliber Colt New Navy pistol at crows in Ned Sanders' corn fields.

Stephen hit the bulls eye each time, and received an 'expert' rating at the end of the day. He was made a shooting instructor the following week.

The next day, Major Witherspoon gave the Officer Candidates a lecture on poison gas at one of the classrooms at Camp Gordon. He began the lecture near a black board, which had the words "phosgene gas," "chlorine gas," and "mustard gas" scrawled thereon.

"Men, one of the most horrible aspects of this war has been the use of poison gas shells by the enemy. They are fired at our lines by German artillery. Sometimes special railway cars are loaded with poison gas canisters, and the cars are backed onto a siding near Allied lines. The Huns then release the gas from the canisters, and attack our lines with a deadly cloud of gas. If you do not have your respirator or gas mask nearby, you can die in seconds. Even if you are partially gassed, you can end up with burnt lungs or blindness, and receive a permanent injury.

"We are going to train you to spot gas attacks, to understand gas alarms, and to properly use your respirators. After classroom instruction, we will take you into a special tent, and expose you to tear gas. You will become proficient in the use of your gas mask equipment. It will become second nature to you.

"We will also train you to kill the enemy when he is approaching in force during a poison gas attack. You must be able to defend your position during such an attack, or you will be overrun. We will also instruct you how to handle your casualties during a gas attack. You must follow proper procedures, or you can easily become a casualty yourself.

"Sergeant Pendergrass, please pass out the textbooks. Gentleman, you will be examined on this material tomorrow. You must pass your written examination if you want to continue your training as an Officer Candidate. Does everyone have a text book? Good. Turn with me to the chart shown on page ten."

The classroom instruction and testing on poison gas warfare lasted five days. Stephen and the other Officer Candidates were then instructed in artillery support, which involved detailed instruction on the 75 mm guns, their military characteristics, and the basic principles of tactics such as the Box Barrage. They were also trained on map coordinates, and how to give coordinates to a Fire Control Officer, in order to give the artillery barrage the maximum effect in its use.

Several days later, Stephen composed another letter to Loralie: Camp Gordon, Georgia

August 6, 1917

Dearest Loralie:

I have been told that we will draw a weekend pass this coming weekend. I will bring Carl with me, and we will catch a train from Rockbridge Station and then up to Elberton. We should depart this camp at three p.m. this Friday.

I am counting the hours when I will be in your arms, love! I have missed you so much. I miss seeing our girls, and hearing their sweet voices. Colonel Harker himself has awarded Carl and I decorations as "Expert" marksman within the past two weeks. We have done over half of our training up to this point.

Tomorrow, a Professor James Davee, a Geography professor from the University of Georgia will give us a lecture on the topography and terrain of the allied section of France where we will be deployed.

Next week love, we will go out with weapons, packs, and field gear, and we will march and bivouac out in the countryside of Gwinnett County. In three weeks, we graduate, and the NCO'S will get their stripes, and the Officers will get their bars.

I have to go now, my love, tattoo is sounding. The only

tenderness allowed in the Army is shown when the bugler blows 'taps' at tattoo. When I get home, I will personally find tenderness with you.

Love,
Stephen

Loralie had several items of business to tend to in Carnesville, the county seat of Franklin County. After the girls got off to school with Ned, she hitched Cherokee to the buggy, and drove out the Black Snake Road toward town. It was mid morning, and it was already getting hot. She tied her straw hat on her head, and kept Cherokee at a brisk pace on the road.

As she neared the turnoff over at the old Brady place, she remembered the lovemaking she had done there with Stephen several months before.

Always one to linger on past thoughts, Loralie impulsively turned Cherokee into the drive. She only wanted to lay her eyes on the oak tree where she and her husband had spent the afternoon in each other's arms.

When she got to the top of the drive, though, she received a surprise. Workmen had torn down the original structure of the Brady home down to the foundation and the driveway, and were hard at work framing out a new structure on the existing foundation.

A tall dark haired man in denim bid overalls walked out from behind a Model T Ford automobile, and greeted Loralie as she dismounted her buggy.

He was young and handsome, and wore an engineer's cap from the Tallulah Falls Railroad. He stepped around one of the carpenters, and helped Loralie down from the buggy.

"To what do I owe the pleasure, ma'am? I'm Mark Lake. I just bought this place from my great aunt. I do not believe we have met before."

Loralie was immediately attracted to this young man, who looked no older than twenty five. She had to give him a pretext for her presence there. "I'm Loralie Harris. I'm one of your neighbors. I just drove by to welcome you to the county. When you get settled in I'll come by and bring you some bread and some jam."

"That's right neighborly of you, ma'am. I'll be busy here on my off days during the week, but after they get done with the house here, I can get out more and see some of the neighbors. I sure would like to call on you sometime."

Loralie had covered her wedding band with her driving glove, and made no effort to tell Mark that she was married. Let Stephen go off and play soldier. She was going to have some fun.

"Please don't take too long, Mr. Lake. You can expect to see me again."

Loralie mounted the buggy, and drove back down the drive to the main road. Her heart was beating wildly in her chest. What was she doing? Her conduct was reckless and flirtatious, but she did not care.

The following weekend, Stephen and Carl Sanders got a weekend furlough, and they caught a train from Norcross to Toccoa. Late Friday night, Ned Sanders met them at the train depot in Toccoa, driving a new model T Ford owned by Mr. Brown.

They drove the thirty five miles from Toccoa to the Black Snake Road in the dark, moonless night, until they arrived home at two in the morning.

Stephen crept in the kitchen door, took off his boots and tip toed to the bedroom in stocking feet. He disrobed at the foot of the bed, and crawled under the cover, and nuzzled Loralie's breast. She welcomed him with a passionate kiss, and Stephen made love to Loralie slowly and passionately. It had been weeks since they had seen one another, and the weeks had gone by like months. She had missed him badly, and he had missed her even more.

The next morning, the girls were surprised to see to see Stephen at the breakfast table. The girls peppered him with questions about the U.S. Army over his bacon and eggs and grits. "What's the Army like, Pa?"

"Well they brought us to the quartermaster when we got to camp, and they examined us with their doctors, and they gave us Army clothes. They took our clothes and mailed them back home at Government expense. We got inoculated for smallpox and typhoid fever. All of our clothing was signed for. Some of the clothing costs will be stopped from our pay."

"When do you get up in the morning?"

"0545. We dress by 0550. We have assembly and roll call at 0600, then we go to the mess hall."

Millie asked more questions.

"What do you eat, Pa?"

"We have grits, eggs, sometimes potatoes, fruit, and coffee. We then fall in for drill from 0645 to 1145 hours. We then go to the mess hall for dinner at 12:15. They cook us meat, potatoes, beans, peas. We get ice water to drink, and we have some kind of dessert, pudding or cake."

Annie asked another question.

"What do you do after dinner?"

"We attend lectures on the Army rules, Articles of War, and warfare. We then clean our rifles, and drill on parade movements, and the manual of arms. We sometimes go out in the field for training in artillery warfare, gas warfare, and we go out to the rifle range at times. We fall in for inspection at 1730 hours, or 5:30 p.m."

"What is the toughest duty you have had so far?"

"K. P, or kitchen police. Man, I hated having to peel potatoes and help prepare meals for a whole company of soldiers."

Loralie reached over Stephen's shoulder, poured him another cup of coffee, and smiled. "Now you know what I have had to put up with over the years, getting meals ready for a bunch of hungry people."

Annie questioned her father some more: "What are you going to do next, Pa? I mean, when you get back to camp?"

"Well, we are to go out and drill in the field with the enlisted men. We will march out somewhere in Gwinnett County and bivouac. We'll go to artillery classes, and we will get some more training with poison gas shells. I have something to show you, though, I'll be right back."

Stephen had on his undershirt, his trousers, and his trench boots. He went into the bedroom and donned his uniform tunic, tucking it into his trousers. He buttoned the blouse up completely, and walked back into the kitchen.

On the edge of his tunic collar, the crossed rifles of the U.S. Army insignia in gold appeared, and underneath, gold U.S. initials shined back at them. On the shoulder straps were silver captain's bars.

Loralie was surprised. "You never told us that you had been promoted, Stephen."

"They had so many draftees come into the camp, that they formed two additional companies in the regiment. I got Company 'I'. Ned was appointed First Sergeant. I got my commission on Thursday, after we graduated from Officer Candidate Class."

Loralie then began asking the questions. "What will you be doing next week, when you return from bivouac?"

"In two weeks, they are going to train us with 3 inch mortars and hand grenades. A Canadian and a British officer will instruct several companies in the regiment on how to knock out German machine gun posts."

"Won't that be an extremely dangerous duty?"

Loralie knew the answer to her question. Stephen had already prepared his answer.

"Yes, but with training and skill, hopefully we can learn to destroy the machine gunners and their posts with minimum risks. We have to train and learn about the enemy tactics, love. We can't just blindly order our men out to die like the British have done over there."

"The newspapers are just full of articles about the killing over there. I am just afraid for you, Stephen."

Stephen walked over and put his hand on her cheek. "Don't be sad right now, love. We haven't even shipped out for France yet. Save your worrying for another day."

"Come on girls, go get dressed. I would like you to show me your Victory Garden."

The girls took Stephen outside, and showed him their summer squash plants, their okra, butterbean rows, carrots, cucumbers, and tomatoes. He helped them hoe the garden that morning, and Loralie made them a big pot of vegetable soup that night.

They ate their soup with hoecake cornbread Stephen fried on the stove. After dark, the girls chased fireflies in the front yard while Stephen held Loralie on the front porch swing.

Loralie was distant. Stephen did not know quite what the problem was, but she was not herself. She even seemed preoccupied when he made love to her late that night.

They got up the next morning, ate a quick breakfast of eggs and ham, and dressed for church. After church, Loralie warmed up the large Sunday dinner she had cooked that morning, Carl and Ned Sanders were invited over to help eat it.

Carl brought his sweetheart to dinner. She was the lovely Sheila McRae. Sheila was wearing a yellow calico dress, a flat white straw hat, and she had deep blue eyes. Stephen knew that she was quite a catch, and wondered what she truly saw in Carl. Carl was just a simple country boy. Sheila had dated several men in Carnesville, and some of them were well to do.

They ate their Sunday dinner slowly, relishing the time that they had together. At three o'clock, Ned loaded their gear into the automobile, and drove them to the train station in Toccoa. The girls cried when Stephen kissed them goodbye, but Loralie seemed distant and preoccupied when Stephen kissed her good bye. Stephen was again puzzled by her behavior. He told them that they probably would not get another weekend pass for a while, but he promised to write them often.

The next Monday afternoon, the girls rode into Royston with Ned to sell a load of melons. Ned promised to pay them each a commission for each melon they sold.

Loralie packed the girls a picnic lunch for the market, and then packed a basket for herself. She hitched Cherokee up to the buggy, and began to drive up toward the Brady place. On the way up the

51

dusty road, she became angry as she thought of Stephen and his eagerness to go to war.

Why was he such a fool? He was abandoning his family, for no good reason it seemed. The Great War had gone on for years, and only a stalemate had resulted.

She was being ignored. He could ignore her and love her, but she was not going to sit still. She would find her some company; and it was not far away.

She drove up to the Brady place, where the contractor and his crew were hard at work on the new home. A moment later, Mark Lake walked up, waving his hand, and Loralie could see the smile on his face from across the yard.

CHAPTER FIVE

The second week in October, 1917, Loralie received another letter from Stephen at Camp Gordon. Early that morning, she cooked breakfast for the girls and packed their lunch baskets with ham and biscuits. Ned drove up in a new GMC truck that he had purchased the month before. He had agreed to drive the girls to school each day, as he now had a contract with the school district that required him to supply most of the schools in the county with milk.

He also made a great deal of money that summer selling corn and forage to the army. He had hired two other boys to do Carl's work, giving him more time to spend with Annie and Millie. Both girls adored him, and loved him as they would their own grandfather.

Loralie had slipped her denim jacket over her nightgown, and stepped out on the front porch to sip her cup of coffee. She waved to Ned out in the driveway, as he helped the girls get seated inside the cap of the GMC truck. She waved also to the girls as Ned pulled down the driveway toward Black Snake Road.

She then opened Stephen's letter and began to read it as the sun began to rise

October 9, 1917
Camp Gordon, Georgia

Dear Loralie:

We have recently begun several weeks of intensive training with our company. We have been selected to receive special training in wiping out German machine gun nests. Our work is hard and tough. Just last week, we had to crawl through tangles of barbed wire, across hog entrails, while machine gunners fired over our heads.

The men did well, though, and we got through that phase of our training without a hitch.

I miss you and the girls terribly. I long to hold you in

my arms, and to kiss your sweet lips. I know in my heart
that you are my true soul mate. I have known that ever
since the first day I laid eye upon you.

Keep the home fires burning for me, honey.

We will get a two week furlough the week of
Christmas. I have to go now, as we are marching
overnight up to Holcomb Bridge Road.

Love,
Stephen

Loralie sipped some more coffee, and peered out at the mountains
shrouded in morning mist. Stephen was such a fool to eagerly join the
Army! He had everything a man could want right in Royston. A good
teaching position, a lovely wife, two lovely children; a paid for
home. Yet he had to go off to war.

She had resented his enlistment so much that her resentment had
influenced her judgment.

After she finished her coffee, she washed her dishes and cleaned
up the kitchen. She then drew and heated some water, and carried it
to the iron and ceramic bathtub in her bathroom.

She stripped her denim jacket and her nightgown, and picked up
her soap and wash rag. She eased down into the warm water, until all
but the tops of her breasts and the tops of her knees were submerged.

She began to slowly bathe, bathing her arms, her legs, her breasts,
and her underarms slowly. She thought about Mark Lake and her
relations she had been having with him. He was handsome, and took
her out to fancy restaurants in Athens and Toccoa at times. He spent
his money lavishly on her. His lovemaking was different from
Stephen's, but she felt wild and alive when she was in Mark's
company.

He had pressed his suit for carnal relations, and she had
succumbed to his charms. She even knew his time schedule at the
railroad, and was aware that he was working the evening shift in
Toccoa.

After she had dressed, she packed a lunch in her basket, along with a jug of milk. She then hitched Cherokee up to the buggy, and drove down the road to Mark's house. He was seated in the yard on a cut log of White Oak, resting after splitting some stove wood with his axe.

Loralie smiled and drew back on Cherokee's reins. Mark was dressed in a black shirt, with blue denim overalls. Loralie was dressed in a navy blue dress, with a yellow straw hat. Mark put his hands around her waist, and lifted her out of the buggy. Loralie gestured toward the lunch basket. "I have lunch packed for us here."

Mark took her by the hand. "Lunch can wait here. I need you right now." He drew her to him, kissed her deeply, and then led her into the house, and into his bedroom.

At Camp Gordon, Stephen formed his company into a group of German machine gunner killers. He had picked men that had played baseball, and taught them how to throw hand grenades. He also worked with the crews that handled the 3 inch trench mortars.

They donned fencing pads, and were taught the fine point of warfare with bayonets. Just before Christmas, Stephen and his company drew two weeks of K.P. duty. In between peeling a mound of potatoes, he wrote Loralie, and told her that they would have a two week furlough the week of Christmas.

When Stephen and Carl got their furlough passes, they had also drawn their Army pay. They went into Norcross, and bought dolls and candy for the girls. Stephen bought Loralie a pretty silver pendant. Carl bought Sheila a diamond ring.

They caught the train up through Gainesville to Cornelia and Toccoa, where Ned met them at the depot in his GMC truck. They caught up on recent news on the ride down to Royston. Ned had taken Millie and Annie up on Buzzard Knob, and had cut them a Christmas tree. Ned picked them a pretty Eastern White Pine. Millie and Annie had decorated it with popcorn chains, tinsel, and hand painted wooden ornaments.

On the way down to Royston, Stephen and Ned discussed

Loralie's recent behavior.

"Ned, what has been eating at Loralie lately? She seemed like she was preoccupied when we came home last time. Have you noticed anything funny about her lately?"

Ned pulled his slouch hat back with his left hand, while he kept his right hand on the steering wheel. "She does go into town a lot during the week. Most of her comings and goings are when the girls are at school, though. She's always home when they get home from school. I agree with you, though. She has been acting funny over the past two months. You need to talk to her, Steve. Just see what might be bothering her."

"I think she is mad about my enlistment. She does not want me to go into the Army."

"Well, if you had not signed up as an officer, you would have been drafted anyway. She needs to understand that you did not have complete control over your military service. Uncle Sam has called the shots on that one."

"We drew our pay from the quartermaster before we left the camp. We bought our girls some nice presents for Christmas. They will be pleased to see all of us, I'm sure."

"Sheila came over to your place last night, so she could help Loralie cook a special dinner for you all. We are all gonna eat high on the hog tonight!"

"I guess she baked a ham and a pecan pie."

"Yeah, she sure did. She made sweet potato soufflé, and she cooked cornbread and cabbage greens. Ms. Beresford over in Carnesville was told you would be home, and she brought over some pecan pralines, and a boiled fruitcake for us, too."

"Sounds like a meal fit for kings. We better enjoy while we can, Carl. This spring, we will be eating canned rations and hard tack at the front, I imagine."

"Yes, sir. We must seize the day, sir, while we can."

"Well said, First Sergeant. Ned, he has made us a very fine NCO. You don't know how proud I am of Carl."

Ned wiped a tear away from his eye as he drove the truck. "Not nowhere near as proud as I am of you both, Steve. You both make very fine soldiers. You just need to return home from this war."

The weather had turned colder in North Georgia that Christmas, and it was almost dark when they pulled down Stephen's drive. Stephen saw a blue streak across the sky, just above the horizon. He spied a plume of white smoke as it wafted up from the driveway. He knew he was almost home, and the thought of spending Christmas with his family brought satisfaction and joy to his heart.

This just might be the last Christmas that he and Carl would have to spend with their loved ones, since they would surely go to war the next spring. Carl was right. Their furlough time was to be savored, and even treasured. As Carl pulled the truck in front of the house, Annie and Millie ran out to hug him, and helped him carry their presents into the house.

Stephen noticed that his cheeks were wet. He then realized that his tears were tears of joy.

As he stepped into the kitchen, he spied Loralie carrying a bowl of boiled cabbage, and he saw her eyes light up as he entered the room in his uniform.

After she had set the bowl on the table, he threw his hat into the corner, and he took her in his arms, and kissed her fully on her lips.

She kissed him back, and then Stephen knew he was truly home.

CHAPTER SIX

Near the end of January, 1918, Loralie learned that she was pregnant. She had sexual relations with both Stephen and Mark Lake during the past six weeks, so the paternity of the child was in question.

She cautiously broke the news to Mark one afternoon before he was to report for his evening shift in Toccoa. He accepted the news calmly. She asked him what should be done about the child, and he advised her that she should carry the child to full term and deliver it, as she had done with Annie and Mille.

How could the paternity situation work out? He advised her that the law would presume the child was Stephen's, unless strict proof to the contrary could be shown in court.

She then wondered about her future life with Stephen. Mark answered her, and told her that those things had to wait until after the war. After all, Stephen had to survive his army adventures in France before her marital problems could be addressed.

Mark kissed her, and held her until it was time for him to leave for Toccoa.

Loralie then sat down and wrote a letter to Stephen about her pregnancy:

February 14, 1918
Capt. Stephen Harris,
Co.I, 325th Inf Regmt.
Camp Gordon, Georgia

Dear Stephen:

This news may take you by surprise, honey. I am going to have another baby. It looks like I will be due around the beginning of September or the end of August, according to Dr. Johnston. I am happy to have another child with you, darling, and I hope that you will return home from the war to help raise him That's right, I believe my woman's intuition tells me that I will bear you a son.

I have heard through the grapevine that you all will get a furlough in March. At that time, I have been told that Carl and Sheila are to be married at our church then. You will be the best man, my love. I will count the days when you will return home to my loving arms.

Your loving wife,
Loralie

March 15th brought a furlough for the men of Company "I," for two weeks, and Carl and Stephen were to make the most of it.

They piled into a train bound for Cornelia after they received their passes. They were in their dress uniforms, with their number two uniforms packed in their duffel bags.

They exited the train when it pulled into Cornelia station, and took a little time to shop for wedding gifts, and a few surprise items for Stephen's girls. Ned drove over to the train station in his GMC truck, and picked them up an hour later.

Stephen and Carl were in their best uniforms, with their broad brimmed campaign hats. Carl's sergeant stripes adorned his sleeves, while Stephen had captain bars on his shoulder straps. The crossed rifle symbols in brass of the U. S. Army appeared on the collars of their tunics. They were now soldiers, and they were fully trained for war.

Ned drove them to a Belk Hudson Department Store, where the men did some quick shopping. Carl brought his bride to be a pretty scarf and a straw hat. Stephen bought Sheila and Carl some dishes, and he bought his bride a hat as well.

He bought some warm knit gloves for the girls, along with some small dolls. They were after all still young girls, and Stephen wanted them to retain their childhood ways, even though the war had placed a strain on their family life.

The following afternoon, Carl and Sheila were married at the

New Pentecostal Church below Royston. Sheila was a beautiful bride. She walked down the aisle of the old white church in a cotton wedding dress with a long train. Carl was in his dress uniform, nervous as a cat about the nuptials. Stephen was the best man.

He stood with Carl at the altar with the Reverend Amos Alexander, a tall fifty five year old pastor, who was dressed in a black frock coat. Stephen looked out at the front row, and spied Loralie and the girls. Loralie was in a crinoline dress of dark blue, and she had her hair pinned up in a bun. Stephen thought that pregnancy agreed with her, as she was radiant and lovely.

He did not understand why she seemed so distant when he returned home on his furlough, though. She had become a riddle and an enigma to him. He could not figure her out. If he lived to be a hundred and three, he would never understand the mysterious ways of woman folk.

After the ceremony, they had a reception at the church social hall, and then the married couple returned to Ned's house for a short honeymoon. Ned was going to bunk in on Stephen's kitchen floor. He drove Stephen, Loralie, and the children home from the church in his GMC truck.

Just after dark, the stars came out a sparkling in the dark and cool night. Loralie and the girls were finishing the dishes while Ned and Stephen walked out onto the front porch. Ned reached into the pocket of his black waist coat, and pulled out small pouch. He removed a briar pipe from the pouch, tamped its bowl full of tobacco, and placed the pipe to his lips. He lit the pipe with a Lucifer match, and began to puff away.

Stephen had become emotional during the wedding ceremony, as he thought about his pregnant wife, and his beautiful daughters. He had experienced a premonition that afternoon; a thought that he was going to die soon. He could not shake off those thoughts. He began to discuss them with Ned.

"Ned, did Pa ever tell you down in Cuba that he did not feel he was coming back?"

Ned stopped pulling on his pipe, and scratched the back of his head.

"No, I don't believe he did. He always talked to us like he was gonna come home to you and your mamma. He never had a clue about getting killed in the war. He always planned on living, you see. It was a stray artillery round that got him, as he was carrying a dispatch down to Lieutenant Pershing when he got hit. It was real sudden. No warning, just a quick explosion after the gun on San Juan Heights fired on us."

"Ned, I have just had a feeling that I may not return back from the war. So many men in Europe have already fallen. I feel like I may not live to see the end of the war."

"Are your affairs in order?"

"I believe so. I purchased life insurance policies earlier. I believe Loralie is pregnant with my son, Ned. I worry about what will happen to her while I am gone. Will you look out for her while I am gone?"

"Sure I will, I will be glad to help you, Steve. You should know that. You go over there and win this war. Don't worry about things here. I will surely look after Loralie while you are gone. I will look in on her and the girls every day."

Stephen put his hand on Ned's shoulder.

"Thank you, Ned. You have lifted a very great burden off of me. I appreciate this more than you will ever know."

"It's nothing, son. I promised your Dad that I would look after you when I got back home after the war, and I keep my promises. You are like a son to me, you know."

Steve placed his hand on Ned's shoulder. "I know, Ned, I have always loved you like a father. In many ways, you have been my father for years. Carl could not have a better father than you."

Ned took two more puffs on his pipe, then stood up and knocked the bowl of the pipe upside down against the porch rail. I guess I better go turn in. The manure is getting deep out here."

Steve laughed, and followed Ned into the house, after he caught a glimpse of the Big Dipper around the corner of the porch.

CHAPTER SEVEN

On May 14, 1918, most of the 325th Infantry Regiment received orders to pack up their gear and march to the train depot, to take the train to Newport News, Virginia. The regiment would then load into transports for the ocean voyage to Europe.

Stephen received sufficient advance notice to allow him to send a Western Union telegram to Ned Sanders in Royston from Norcross:

Western Union
May 5, 1918

To: NED SANDERS
From: CAPT. STEPHEN HARRIS, 325TH INFANTRY DIVISION

OUR TRAIN LEAVING ROCKBRIDGE STATION FOR ATHENS 5/16/18 AT 0750 HOURS STOP WILL ARRIVE IN ELBERTON AT APPROX. 1450 HOURS ON SAME DATE STOP CAN YOU BRING SHEILA, LORI AND GIRLS TO MEET US AT STATION SAME DATE AND TIME IN ELBERTON? STOP NEED TO SEE THEM ALL.

STEVE

They were later loaded into Army GMC trucks, and were driven from Norcross down to the Rockbridge train station early the next morning. Their weapons and gear were packed into crates, and their uniforms and mess kits were stowed in their knapsacks and haversacks.

They marched in company formation out to the waiting trucks, and then they rode the eight miles down to Rockbridge Station.

Officers and NCOs from all over the regiment had sent telegrams out to friends and relatives from all over the area, and they appeared at each station on the way to greet the departing soldiers.

Women and pretty girls waved their hats and small American flags at each stop, and men and boys shouted and cheered them at each station they passed.

Stephen looked out the window of his car, seated next to Ned, and observed the beautiful spring countryside of North Georgia. He knew those red clay hills better than most, and he loved them dearly. Would this be the last time he would see them? He pondered these questions in his heart as he rode the train from Athens over to Comer, and then on to Elberton.

As luck would have it, the coal fired locomotive *Robert Toombs* which pulled their train was scheduled for coaling and a water stop at Elberton.

Just after they had finished their meal of cold corned beef and cold coffee, the *Robert Toombs* pulled into the Elberton train station. Stephen could see the cupola of the large courthouse from the edge of the train station. The conductor passed from car to car, and advised the men that they would be stopped to re-coal and water for thirty minutes. Any soldier who needed to use the privy or stretch his legs could do so now.

As was the case at the other station, a crowd of locals was waiting to greet the departing native sons aboard the train. Stephen put his pack and haversack on his seat, and exited out the rear of the passenger car. As he mounted the wooden platform at the station, he spied the wooden side body of Ned's GMC truck.

He saw Carl running over to Sheila, hugging and kissing her on both cheeks. He then saw Annie and Millie running toward him in their Sunday dresses, with their blonde hair billowing behind them.

He hugged his lovely daughters and kissed them, and then walked over to the cab of the truck where Ned was helping Loralie down. She was six months pregnant, and was beginning to show. Stephen thought she looked lovely in her forest green crinoline dress. She had on a straw hat with a green ribbon, and the tears were beginning to stream their way down her cheeks.

Stephen took her in his arms and then kissed her, and told her that he loved her. He hugged Millie and Annie again, and they reached into a basket, and began to pass him small items of food wrapped in wax paper.

Loralie wiped her face with her handkerchief and began to explain. "I made you and Carl some ham and biscuits to eat on the way. Ned and Sheila brought you some cheese and crackers to eat on the ship when you get to your port. Where will you board your ship?"

Stephen told her that they were to sail for France from Newport News, Virginia.

"We'll be on this train another two days getting there, but we sail for France right away."

They were not at the train station very long, and Stephen knew that their time was short. He bent down and whispered to the girls. "I need to sweet talk your mother for a few minutes, and then I'll come back to say good bye to you." Millie's face turned red in protest, but Annie took her by the hand and led her over to where Carl and Sheila were standing. They wanted to say good bye to Carl before he boarded the Pullman car.

Stephen whispered into Loralie's ear. "I had almost forgotten how beautiful you are when you are pregnant. I remember one night we had together when you were pregnant with Annie. Motherhood becomes you, darling."

Loralie blushed when she was reminded of their lovemaking. "Stop it, Stephen, don't speak of such things in front of all these people, let alone our own children."

He decided then that the talking had to stop. He had to let his actions demonstrate what was in his heart. He grabbed Loralie about her waist, and kissed her deeply. He looked deeply into her eyes as she drew away from his face, and he began to speak.

"You just take good care of our son, darling. I will return home to our family once we end this war. You take care of yourself and our children. Just remember that I have always loved you."

He turned away from Loralie and went over to kiss his blonde haired daughters good bye. They cried in his arms and told him how much they would miss him, and he began to notice that tears were welling up in his eyes as well. He kissed the girls one last time, and then turned and hugged Ned Sanders, his old friend. "Ned, you take care of our girls while we are gone. We will return after we win this war. God bless you for being so good to us."

Ned shook his hand as he stepped onto the steps of the Pullman car.

"You take care of your men, Stephen, and take care of yourself, too. I'll watch out for the womenfolk while you are gone."

The *Robert Toombs'* whistle blew two blasts, and the conductor shouted, "All aboard!" as the wheels on the Pullman car began to move forward. Stephen took one last look at Loralie, Ned, Sheila and the girls as the train lurched forward from the station. They were waving their handkerchiefs at him in the spring breeze. Tears were streaming down each of their faces.

He knew that the time would come for him to leave for Europe. He then realized that he had run out of time to see his family, and he could only hope that he would survive the war and see them again. He went back to his seat on the Pullman car, where he shared a seat with Carl. They soon crossed the Savannah River into South Carolina. The train was filled with troops of the 82nd Division, and there was no room for them in the sleeping berths. Carl and Stephen drew straws for the first opportunity to sleep on the floor of the car, and Carl got the short straw. He soon stretched out on the floor of the car with his blanket, while he used his rolled up poncho for a pillow. Stephen switched on his reading lamp on in his seat, and began to study President Woodrow Wilson's Fourteen Points speech from an old copy of the *Atlanta Constitution*.

Stephen began to get drowsy, and soon fell asleep, as he remembered the lovely sight of Loralie's naked breasts during their lovemaking. He dreamed of being in bed with her, and being home in Royston with his children.

The *Robert Toombs* carried the regiment to Greenwood, and then on to Columbia and Florence, South Carolina. They made a long stop below Fayetteville to re-coal and to take on water early the next morning. Stephen and Carl used the stop to visit the privy, and to eat the ham and biscuits Loralie had fixed for them. The train got underway an hour later, and they went through Raleigh, Durham, and on to Weldon.

Late in the afternoon, they arrived in Weldon, and at eight o'clock, the *Robert Toombs* went through Petersburg. At nine thirty, the train was routed into the Richmond station, and onto a railroad line headed down the James Peninsula, and into Newport News.

At one o'clock, the *Robert Toombs* arrived at the Newport News station, where they were ordered to exit the train, and to assemble in a bivouac area in a large field. The men had trouble navigating by moonlight, but reported with all of their equipment. They were ordered to march from the field down to the waterfront, where they boarded a transport under the illumination of large kerosene lanterns. It took two hours for the entire 325th Infantry Regiment to board the U.S.S. *Narragansett*, a large two stack ocean steamer.

They stowed their gear in their bunks below, and sacked out until 0600 hours the next morning.

The next morning, after morning mess, Stephen began a history lesson to some of the men of the company as the steamer tugs pulled the U.S.S. *Narragansett* out into Hampton Roads. Carl watched Stephen instruct the men about the C.S.S. *Virginia's* attack on the U.S.S. *Congress* and the U.S.S. *Cumberland* during the Civil War.

Stephen then told the men about the artillery duel the following day between the C.S.S. *Virginia* and the U.S.S. *Monitor*.

While Stephen was talking, a tall naval officer in the navy blue uniform of a lieutenant approached them. Stephen noticed his presence at once.

"I'm sorry, sir, did I delay you in carrying out your duties?"

The naval lieutenant denied any wrong doing on Stephen's part.

"Oh, no. I just love to hear naval history, especially local naval history on this area. I am required to instruct the men on the use of life vests and man ropes in the event we are struck by a torpedo from a U-Boat."

"Please proceed, lieutenant. I did not get your name."

"Stackhouse, Lieutenant James Stackhouse."

Lieutenant Stackhouse instructed the men of Company I in the proper use of a life vest and in the process of leaving or entering the ship if it was attacked by a U-Boat. He then took Stephen off to the taffrail and began to quietly give him some additional information.

Stephen motioned, and began to instruct the soldiers.

"First, there is to be no smoking on the open deck, especially at night or in the early morning hours. That light makes a target for a German U-Boat.

"Second, if any of the deck guns are knocked out of action by enemy fire from the surface, Army personnel would be used to get the guns back into action."

The convoy was to form just beyond Hampton Roads, with nine transports, one destroyer, two escorts, and five sub chasers. They would sail a zig zag course across the Atlantic to Liverpool.

Stephen also instructed the men about their rations. "You are to mess aboard ship until we make the English Channel.

"You will then be issued traveling rations to tide us over until we cross over to France.

"Do not eat up your travel rations right away. It might be quite a while before we get to our billets in France. If you eat your travel rations up, your may not eat again for a while."

Stephen asked Carl to dismiss the men, and then joined a group of officers at the rail. Colonel Harker pointed out the small sub chasers that were speeding around the outside of the convoy. The sub chasers were 110 feet long, were built mostly of wood, and they were very fast, with three Standard gasoline powered engines. Stephen watched a sub chaser speed past their port bow, and he noticed its guns and torpedo tubes on the deck. He saw the sailor on deck waving at the men aboard the *Narragansett*. He looked to the stern of the ship, and saw the transport *Mount Vernon* and its two smoke stacks through the morning mist.

Colonel Harker told them that the sailors would commence boat drills that afternoon, and invited Stephen to a poker game in the officer's wardroom. Stephen politely declined the card game, but did accept an invitation to dine with the officers at evening mess. Stephen ate dinner at 3:30 p.m. with several of the naval officers in the wardroom. The ship's crew only served two meals a day.

Breakfast was served between nine and ten o'clock, and dinner could be served anywhere from 3 to 5 o'clock p.m. The conversation around the wardroom mess centered on the German offensive launched with 40 divisions in March on the Western Front.

A number of Stephen's men of the company were sea sick, and could not stand the rolling of the ship once the convoy reached the rollers of the North Atlantic. Stephen had gone to sea before on his honeymoon. He had sailed with Loralie from Savannah to New York aboard the Cunard steamer the *Star of India*, so he was used to the rolling of a ship at sea.

Stephen had a cast iron stomach, and could eat all manner of army and navy food, whether it was steaming hot, ice cold, or lukewarm. His cast iron stomach served him well in Uncle Sam's Army.

After the evening mess, the officers went to the end of wardroom to play cards and other games of chance.

Stephen returned to his bunk, where he drafted a long letter to Loralie.

During the next week, Stephen would commence a routine in the mornings of observing the ships in the convoy, and using his field glasses to scan the horizon for the periscope of a German U-Boat. They watched the sailors participate in boat drills, and on two occasions, were treated to prize fights which were put on by the navy officers and some of the army enlisted men.

On June 24, the convoy safely arrived at Liverpool harbor, and the men and their equipment were landed by British steam lighters.

They marched three miles to Knotty Branch, where the British Army had established a camp known as a rest camp. The rest camp was stocked with a section of cold showers, a nurses' aide station, and tents known as canteens where hot food was served.

The only rest that the men received at rest camp was on their stomachs, as the rations were not agreeable to most of the men. One afternoon when Stephen was in line to receive his ration at the rest camp, Carl Sanders returned his way with a steaming mess kit full of soup, a cup of hot tea, and cheese and crackers. Upon recognizing Stephen's face, Carl began to describe their afternoon ration.

"Sir, just look at these rations. No wonder the Brits are losing this war. I've got some watery piss-poor oxtail soup, some moldy cheese, a couple of crackers, and some old tea to drink. Sir, we got here just in the nick of time. Another couple of months on these rations, and these Brits surely would have lost this war."

Stephen was amused at the observations of Carl Sanders about the British rations, but he issued orders to the company for the men to save their travel rations of canned tomatoes, salmon, and beans for their travel into France.

Two days later, they were marched in column to the stock yards near Knotty Branch and loaded aboard a small passenger train. They steamed on to Southampton, where they detrained, and marched three or four miles in columns out to the commons, where they loaded aboard steam lighters, and were carried out to a converted steam passenger liner that Stephen recognized as the *Star of India*.

Late that afternoon, the *Star of India* weighed anchor, and took them around to Spithead, the Dungeness, the North Foreland, and then up the Thames River into London. They were ordered to climb down a specially rigged cargo net into small lighters, which began to take them further up the Thames into London. Stephen and the entire 325th Infantry Regiment had been given the honor of parading before King George V himself. The soon passed the Tower of London, London Bridge, and Somerset House.

Stephen was thrilled that they would land at Whitehall, and would march up past the Horse Guards before King George V. They disembarked and climbed Whitehall Steps, while the ebb tide was running full, and Stephen could see the mud on either side of the Thames. They were in their full field pack and gear, and wore their campaign hats. Like a dream, they assembled in company formation, and then began to march past the Admiralty House, past the Horse Guards, the Prime Minister's residence on 10 Downing Street, and they turned and marched past the Houses of Parliament.

Crowds of men in bowler hats, and women in dark dresses cheered them as they marched in formation up Great George Street, and past St. James Park. A reviewing stand had been constructed for King George V, and the soldiers saluted him as they marched past his Majesty's stand. Stephen saw a familiar figure in a top hat near King George, and he was later told that it was the Assistant Secretary of the Navy, Franklin D. Roosevelt.

They marched through cheering crowds past Charing Cross, past the old tall buildings of London, and then up Pall Mall, and then the column turned up St. James street. The crowds were waving British and American flags, and they were constantly cheering. They turned down Piccadilly Street, and up to Piccadilly Circus, where Stephen saw many red, funny looking double decked busses for the first time.

Like a dream, they soon marched past Trafalgar Square, and then back to Whitehall Steps, where they boarded the lighters. After they boarded the *Star of India* at Wapping, they sailed past the North Foreland, and down and across the English Channel to LeHavre, France.

The Loire River was wide and deep at LeHarve harbor, and the three transports could pull up directly to the quay and disembark troops. Once the men disembarked from the ships at LeHavre, they marched past Negro stevedores and porters that Stephen recognized as U.S. troops in the Services of Supply. It was their duty to unload the supplies for the front line combat soldiers.

They then marched another three miles to another rest camp known as Rest Camp Number 3 near LeHavre Harbor.

The men had better rations at the British run rest camp at LeHavre. Several hours later, they marched two kilometers to the train station, where they were loaded aboard train cars affectionately know as "40x8's." Each car was known as 40's and 8's because they could either carry 40 men per car, or 8 horses per car. The box cars contained wooden stalls that could be put up to separate horses, or they could be taken down to accommodate men. The men were loaded into these cars and packed tightly.

No sanitary arrangements were made for the men, and the men had to relieve themselves whenever the train stopped to take on water or coal.

The cars had no room for the men to sleep or to lay down, so the men slept standing up while the train rolled eastward. After traveling for twenty-eight hours on the miserable steam train, the train unloaded the men in Menancourt, France.

Once in town, each of the companies were ordered to report to a French Major who was known as a Town Major. For the first time since the Napoleonic War, foreign troops were billeted on French soil. The Town Major would write out in chalk before each house the number of troops that may be quartered at each residence. The men formed up in columns before the train station, and marched into town in company formation. Near the town gates, Stephen spied children who had picked flowers for them, and were throwing flowers at the soldiers as they marched before them.

Menancourt was lovely little country town, and Stephen and Carl and five of their men were billeted in a large farm house near a dairy at the edge of town. They were fed by a local French woman, who made them a hearty breakfast of French bread and eggs and pork. Stephen and Carl were informed that they were staying at the home Monsieur Pierre LaPrawn. Pierre was sixty years of age, and had a permanent limp, that he received at Sedan in 1871 from a Prussian needle gun. His wife Marie, was a lovely forty-two year old woman with auburn hair and freckles. Their son had been killed at Verdun, but their daughter Mozelle was a twenty year old nurse at Chaumont.

Every Monday, Marie would wash and press the men's Army uniforms, and every Saturday, Stephen would hold company inspection in front of the Town Square. The people in Menancourt loved the soldiers, and were proud of Stephen and his company.

CHAPTER EIGHT

In August, back in Royston, Loralie was shelling purple hull peas on her porch when she felt a sharp pain between her legs.

She then saw her water as it oozed out onto the wooden floor of the front porch. She cried for Annie, who was in the kitchen making biscuits.

Annie ran out onto the porch, and saw her mother pulling at her wet skirt.

"Tell Millie to come out here and help me over to the bedroom. She will need to put some water on to boil. You need to saddle Cherokee and go get Ned. He has to drive to Toccoa to get the doctor."

Annie ran as fast as her nine year old frame could let her. She found Millie near the root cellar, and told her that Loralie needed her. She then streaked out to the paddock behind the barn, grabbing Cherokee's bridle from a peg near his stall.

She had on her denim overalls, and her hair was plaited in pigtails. She had laced up her brogans tightly that morning, though, because she thought something was about to happen that morning. She was right!

She caught Cherokee quickly, and had his bridle on and his bit in his mouth in a few moments. She climbed on his back, riding bareback, and pressed her knees against his flanks. He then set off at a trot for Ned Sander's farm up the road.

The summer heat from the dog days had begun to set in that morning, and Annie noticed the Katydids as they began their singing in the trees off the road.

As she rounded a bend in the road, she saw Ned out in the hayfield, raking hay. She rode up to a gate near the wire field fence, dismounted, and opened the gate for Cherokee. After she had negotiated the gate, she remounted, and led Cherokee at a smart trot up to Ned's hay field. Ned saw her coming, and he stopped his mule and his hay rake. He wiped the dust and sweat from his brow, and asked Annie what was wrong. Annie told him that Loralie was in labor. Ned turned his mule over to his hired hand. He gave him some instructions, and rode Cherokee double with Annie up to the house.

He hitched Cherokee up to his old wagon, and sent Annie into the house to find Sheila. Sheila was in the kitchen making soup. She was already showing herself, Annie noticed, but she still looked beautiful, even though she was also expecting.

Sheila gathered up some things into a basket, and loaded up into the wagon with Annie.

Ned told them that he was driving over to Toccoa to find the doctor. He grabbed his flask of water, and a box of cheese and crackers, and headed out to his GMC truck, kissing Sheila on the cheek as he passed her.

He had just refueled the truck that morning after his milk run into Royston, in anticipation of being summoned by Loralie. He then drove the GMC truck through the hills of North Georgia toward Toccoa, and Dr. Emory Johnston.

Loralie got to her bed when her water broke, with Millie's assistance. She directed Millie to boil some water on the stove, and to round up a number of towels. Loralie could feel the sharp labor pains, and she began to time her contractions with her father's old pocket watch.

She only hoped that Ned could arrive with some assistance, and a trained physician.

When Ned arrived in Toccoa almost two hours later, he was detained by a nurse at the front desk of the clinic.

"Doctor Johnston is operating on two Federal Revenue Agents. They were hit with buckshot while serving an arrest warrant on a moonshiner."

Ned was now in a state of panic. "But I have an emergency. I have a woman in labor down in Royston. How much longer can Doc Johnston be in surgery?"

The nurse was around thirty years old, with blue eyes and curly dark hair. She had her curly hair pinned back in a bun.

"He just started on those men a half hour ago. They were hit on the back, and Doctor Johnston must take out each of the shot pellets. He will have those men in surgery for at least two hours."

Ned was now in a near state of panic. He began to breathe rapidly, and tried to think of what else he could do.

"Isn't there some other doctor in this area? Or even a good midwife?"

The nurse did have a suggestion.

"There is a lady that runs a tavern just south of Lavonia. It is called the Swamp Guinea. She has been a midwife around here for years. If I were you, I would go and get her to go back to Royston with you. Lavonia is on your way back anyhow. Her name is Granny Mat Mason."

Ned thanked the nurse for her time, and ran out the front door of the clinic. He spun the crank on his GMC truck, and stomped the accelerator as he eased out the clutch. He had to find that midwife in Lavonia. There was not a moment to be lost.

Forty minutes later, Ned saw the facade of an old split lumber tavern near the side of the road. He remembered the place, as he and William Harris had gone there to drink beer just before they enlisted in the Rough Riders.

He pulled the truck around the side of the building, and entered the dimly lit tavern. He saw some lumberjacks drinking beer at a table in the corner of the room. They were being waited on by a slim dark haired girl of twenty years. The girl was blue eyed, and wore a low cut frilly dress.

Ned was all business. "Excuse me, Miss, but where can I find Granny Mat?"

The girl stopped pouring beer from her pitcher, and looked up. "She's in the kitchen, fixing those men a sandwich."

"Could you please get her for me, I have a woman in labor that needs her real bad."

"Yes, sir." The girl quickly stepped back into the kitchen, and emerged a couple of minutes later with a fifty five year old woman with jet black hair. She was slim, but curvaceous, and wore a black dress with a cameo, and puffed sleeves. Her jet black hair was in a tight bun, and she wore a straw hat.

"You have some business with me, Mister?"

Ned stepped toward her.

"Yes, madam. I'm Ned Sanders, from down near Royston. I have a neighbor lady who is in labor, and Doc Johnston is unavailable. I am in dire need of your services."

The woman pulled a old corn cob pipe from her apron, and placed it in her mouth.

"All the way to Royston, huh? Well, sir, that will cost you. I'll have to get Bonnie Sue to close my establishment early while I am gone. It will run you at least eight dollars."

"I have that in my pocket ma'am. Do you have a bag or kit to bring with you? We really need to get going."

"Bonnie Sue will get if for me. I am at your service, sir."

"We need to get moving quickly, ma'am. There is not a moment to be lost."

Almost an hour later, Ned's GMC truck came roaring down Stephen's drive. Ned pulled around to the back of the house, and helped Granny Mat through the kitchen to Loralie's bedroom. Sheila met them at the door.

"Where's Doc Johnston?" she asked.

"He is operating on two Federal Revenue Agents that got shot. His nurse recommended Granny Mat Mason here. She's a mid wife, and she came to help us."

Granny Mat took off her hat, and got down to business at once. "How far apart are her labor pains, honey?"

Sheila answered at once. "About nine minutes, now." Granny Mat looked around the kitchen, and surveyed all that had been laid out for the delivery. "Get me some sharp scissors, honey, some twine, and a few more towels. This baby will be coming pretty soon."

Ned had to go milk his cows, and he returned to the house three hours later. When he arrived in the kitchen, he found Sheila and the girls running around with smiles on their faces.

"Has the baby come yet?"

Sheila was bursting with news.

"Those girls have a baby brother. Loralie just named him Matthew Clayton Harris. He arrived about an hour ago?"

"Where's Granny Mat?"

"She's helping Loralie clean up a bit. Loralie is nursing the baby right now, too."

"When can I see him?"

"In a few minutes. He needs to finish his first meal."

Twenty minutes later, Granny Mat emerged from the bedroom with a bundle up in her arms. Ned walked over and pulled the towel back, to see a small dark haired infant, cooing and twisting in his wrappings.

"Thank you Granny Mat for coming. You were a big help to us all today. How is Loralie?"

"She is doing fine. Sheila fixed some soup for her, and she should take that right away."

"I fixed you some coffee, Granny Mat, just the way you like it, according to what you told me." Sheila handed her a steaming cup. "I have some coffee for you, too, Papa Ned."

Ned thanked her for the coffee, and asked Granny Mat if she would like to take her coffee with him on the front porch.

When they got to the front porch, Ned settled up with her right away. He gave her eight dollars, plus an additional dollar for her short notice summons to duty.

Granny Matt pulled a corncob pipe from her apron, and began to stuff it with tobacco she pulled from a leather pouch at her apron. She lit the pipe with a Lucifer match she struck on the porch post, and began to enjoy the pipe with her coffee.

"This boy's Pa will be proud when he gets off his shift with the railroad."

Ned was tired and groggy, but he was not that groggy. He looked at her over his coffee cup. "Railroad, what are you talking about?"

"I thought Lori was married to a railroad engineer from around these parts. Tall, dark haired man. I have seen him with Lori every other Tuesday and Thursday up at my place. I have served them myself. They would eat dinner, and I seen 'em kissin' and lovin' on one another. I thought they was married."

Ned knew that this was a serious situation, and it had to be dealt with discreetly. "Granny Mat, this needs to be our little secret. Lori is married to a man by the name of Stephen Harris. He is now over in France. He was a schoolteacher, but now he is a captain in the Army."

"You mean while her husband has been serving Uncle Sam, this hussy has been making time with another man? Hell, I seen it with my own two eyes. That boy in there may not even be his."

"Granny Mat, I can't let this little secret of ours get out. At least until Stephen returns home from France anyway."

"What is your real name, anyway?"

"Martha Jane Mason. But they call me Granny Mat."

"Will you swear to me that you won't breathe a word about what we talked about to anyone, at least until I can contact her husband?"

"Yes, I will. I ain't no home wrecker anyway. All of this will come out in the wash when her husband gets back home."

"Thank you. Let's get you back up to the Swamp Guinea. I want to buy a beer from you when we get there. After what I just heard, I may even need to get a shot of whiskey."

Granny Mat just laughed, as they loaded up into Ned's GMC truck.

Ned drove Granny Mat back home to the Swamp Guinea, where he had a beer. At the bar, he pondered over the child's paternity. Stephen had gotten leave both in November and December. Lori had been with the railroad engineer some then, too, he figured. Both men had access to her around the time of the child's conception.

As he drove back to Royston, an idea crept into his head. Stephen's second toe was long and crooked, like a coconut palm tree. If the infant boy had a crooked second toe, surely he would be Stephen's son. He could then confront Lori about her affair, and ask her to break off her relationship with the engineer. Stephen would then have his family intact when he returned home from the war.

But what if the child was not his? Ned came to the conclusion that if the child had a straight second toe, he was probably not Stephen's, and he would then have a duty to disclose the affair to Stephen. Any dispute about the boy's paternity could then be settled in the courts.

As Ned drove back home, he felt relieved that he had prepared a plan of action. He needed to see the infant as soon as possible, and take a good look at his feet. He could only pray that he was doing the right thing in helping an absent Stephen deal with his family problems.

The next day, Ned drove over to Stephen's farm house, where he assisted Annie in milking the cow. Sheila had cooked them a large ham the day before, so Ned sliced and fixed the girls some ham and eggs for their breakfast.

Loralie was too weak to take her meal in the kitchen, so Ned had Annie take a breakfast tray into her bedroom.

Ned soon had an opportunity to take close look at little Matthew Clayton.

Annie took him out to sponge him off with a damp sponge, and Ned held him while Annie wiped him dry with a towel, and wrapped him in a soft blue blanket.

Ned looked at Matthew's toes carefully for a moment. The second toe from the big toe on each foot was perfectly straight, and was not crooked in the least.

Ned took another close look at Matthew's little feet, and then informed Loralie that he had to go finish getting in his hay. He promised to return with Sheila that evening, as Sheila was going to cook them up anther fine meal.

Ned was shaking as he started his truck and drove back to his hayfield. He spent some of the afternoon raking and baling hay with the hands. But he then returned to the house to his study.

At his desk, he pondered over a letter that he knew he had to write to Stephen. He loved Loralie and the girls, but Stephen was like a son to him. He had watched William Harris die in Cuba, and he had sworn to look after Stephen all of his life. He did not want to send

Stephen any letters that would erode his will to fight the war, but he believed that he owed him the truth concerning Matthew's paternity. What would he want of if the roles were reversed and he was at the front?

He would only want to know the truth.

Ned grabbed his pen, dipped it into his inkwell, and began a letter to Stephen on his stationery:

August 15, 1918
Capt. Stephen Harris
325th Infantry Regmt.
Company "I"
APO AEF
France

Dear Stephen,

I take pen in hand to bring you news of great importance. Yesterday, Loralie give birth to a boy baby, who appears to weigh around eight pounds. He is dark haired and green eyed, and very healthy. Loralie has named him Matthew Clayton Harris.

I could not get the doctor to come, as he was in surgery, but I got a nurse midwife from Lavonia to deliver the child. She runs an establishment near Lavonia called the Swamp Guinea. She told me after she delivered the child that she had seen Loralie and a young railroad engineer together in her tavern at least once a week during the past nine months.

This woman appears to be reliable and credible. She told me that Loralie and the engineer were kissing and holding hands most of the time they were dining at her tavern. She believed them to be intimate, and assumed that the engineer was the boy's father. She also believed the engineer resided somewhere near Royston. She also told me that Loralie was fine, and experienced a normal delivery, without complications.

Stephen, I have known you all of your life. I would never tell you anything to deliberately upset you, or to harm you and your family in any way. I only have your best interest at heart.

However, I felt an obligation to convey information to you that the paternity of your son is in question. When you return home from the war, you deserve the opportunity to investigate Loralie's infidelity, and take whatever action you deem appropriate and just.

Please do your best to fight the Germans, end the war, and return home to us. I will look after your family until you can return.

Your good and faithful friend,
Ned

P.S. Please remember that I have always loved you as I loved my own son. Say hello to Carl for me. Sheila sends her love to you both.

CHAPTER NINE

In the middle of August, Carl Sanders found Stephen and advised him that a courier had summoned him to Colonel Charles Harker's command post, which was located at the Menancourt Inn. Stephen saluted the sentries at the door, and reported to the assembly room, where he had a brief conversation with Major Richard Mabry, the deputy commander, and Captain Frank Fish, who commanded Company "C."

The regimental Sergeant Major was a wiry thirty seven year old mountain man from Clayton, Georgia by the name of Waymon Sims.

Waymon was a legend in the Army, as he fought with Teddy Roosevelt's "Rough Riders," at San Juan Hill. Waymon single-handedly killed to two Spanish gun crews with his specially equipped Krag Jorgenson rifle, and a telescopic sight.

Colonel Harker admired him, and allowed him to open every officer's call with the telling of a funny story. Waymon insisted that Lt. Colonel Theodore Roosevelt ran his officer's call the same way during the Spanish American War, and Colonel Harker decided that he would carry on that tradition in this war.

Sergeant Major Sims called the assembly to order, and then began the telling of another funny story:

"My daddy knew a man in Gainesville who sold and traded horses and mules by the name of O.B. Williams. When I was twelve years old, my daddy took me down to Gainesville one spring to buy some watermelon seeds and chicken feed.

"We went over to Williams' lot, where a Negro man was eye-balling a big long eared gray mule. Mr. Williams was singing the mule's praises to the old Negro, who was watching the mule's every move.

"The old Negro saw something that he didn't like, and told Mr. Williams, 'But, Mr. Williams, dat mule's blind. I just seen him step in a hole.'

"Mr. Williams had an answer for everything, and he was never to be cheated out of a sale. He spat out some tobacco juice from his quid in his mouth, and did not miss a lick.

"He told the old Negro, 'Aw, he's not blind, he just don't give a damn'."

The men in the assembly room all laughed, and Sergeant Major Sims then turned the floor over to Colonel Harker. The colonel strolled up the podium, took out his notes, as he began to speak to the officers of the 325th Infantry Regiment.

"Men, we have received orders to advance to the St. Mihiel Salient. We will support the attack of the 82nd Division, which will be launched from the banks of the Moselle River, northward in a drive to Sedan. The First Corps will deploy along a front from Pont-a-Mousson, to the town of Limey. We will attack along a heavily wooded area through the Moselle River, and will drive due north. Our forward objective is the railroad junction town of Metz along the Moselle River.

"You will issue orders for your companies to form tomorrow morning at 0600 hours, and they will load on the railroad cars.

"A light rail line has been constructed from Reims to Verdun, and thence from there to St. Mihiel. From just below St. Mihiel, you will load onto transfer trucks, and you will be trucked to a point east of the town of Limey. You will march to the jump off position near Pont-a-Mousson, and you will draw most of rifle and mortar ammunition at that point. The men will be issued extra ammo once they reach the end of the line, and helmets will be issued at that time as well.

"You men are some of the best that we have in the Army. You have been training for this moment. I expect you to do your best. That is all, you are dismissed."

Stephen took out his order book, and issued a written march order for First Sergeant Carl Sanders to issue to the company. He then hiked back to his hut near his billet that served as Company Headquarters, and asked Carl to copy the order for each of the platoon sergeants, and have the muster assembly and roll call at 0500 hours, and to prepare to march at 0530 hours to the rail head.

It is time for them to get into the war, and to take their position for the coming attack.

CHAPTER TEN

Stephen packed his mess kit, weapon, and gear, and began to move out in the direction of the train station. The entire company got ready to move, and one hour later they marched down to the train station, where they again boarded the 40X8 cars.

The train took them east, in the direction of St. Mihiel, near the terminus of the railhead at Loudmont. The light rail cars carried them to a point near Loudmont, where they reached the end of the line.

They detrained, and loaded aboard French trucks, for a short drive along a motor way that paralleled the front, until the roadway ended just east of the small town of Limey.

The men were then unloaded off the trucks, and were required to report to the quartermaster, who had set up the 82nd and the 90th Divisions and the 2nd and 5th Divisions nearby.

Each of the men were issued an several bandoleers of Enfield rifle ammunition, and an M1917 steel helmet. The men serving the trench mortars were issued ammunition for their three inch Stokes mortars. The machine gunners were issued machine gun ammunition at that time also. Their other equipment had already been issued to them in England.

The men marched approximately three and one half miles to their jump off point near the front, to the small town of Pont-a-Mousson. Stephen noticed many unusual things when he got to the front. First, the entire area in front of the dugouts and no man's land was utterly devoid of vegetation. Most of the large trees had been shot away by either allied or German artillery, or by gunfire. Poison gas had destroyed what ever vegetation remained on either small bushes or trees. It had rained the day before, and the shell holes and craters that had been created by the explosive ordinance and artillery had caused the ground to collect water, and created a huge sea of mud across the front. The mud was everywhere, in the trenches, in the dugouts, and in the traverse trenches at the rear of the front.

Stephen's nose was besieged by an odorous symphony emanating from the dugout. The dugout smelled of mule dung, human feces and urine, rat feces and urine, vomit, muddy soil, canned food, and unwashed human bodies. His journey to the front was one of the most sickening experiences of his life.

On September 11, 1918, a courier came forward from Colonel Harker's dugout, summoning all the company officers to an officer's call. Stephen made sure that his pencil and small notebook were securely in his pocket, and he began the short journey from his company's dugout to the command post of Colonel Harker.

Carl stopped Stephen while he was on his way to the officer's call and handed him a letter from Ned Sanders.

Mail call was earlier that morning, and Carl simply held Stephen's letter for the purpose of presenting to him later that day. Stephen did not have time to read the letter, so he shoved it into the side pocket of his uniform, and eased up the trench to Colonel Harker's dugout.

Major Richard Mabry, the politician from Madison County, had been appointed Chief of Staff for Colonel Harker. He was nothing more than a paper pusher, Stephen thought, but a war record would enhance his chances of being elected to Congress when he returned home after the war.

Major Mabry called the meeting to order, and allowed Sergeant Major Sims to open the conference with another funny story.

"My Pa went down to Dewey Rose, Georgia and bought a giant white faced bull, and had two teams of horses pull him up to our farm on a big trailer. He was huge, and I piled up and composted his manure, and began to grow vegetables using the compost as a fertilizer.

"The butterbeans I planted got huge to the point where two or three beans picked off from the bush would provide a full meal to a grown man."

Carl Sanders could not help but ask the loaded question: "What happened to your bull, sergeant major?"

"He died. His pecker was too large for our heifers, and they would not breed with him, so he died from a case of blue balls."

The men laughed, and Colonel Harker got down to business. He checked his pocket watch, and noticed it was now after six o'clock p.m. Once all of the company officers were present, Colonel Harker turned up the kerosene lantern on his table, and began to unfold a map of the entire front covering the St. Mihiel salient. "Men, we will attack on the American right flank with the rest of the 82nd Division.

"Our objective is to attack and conquer Hill No. 42, which has been fortified by the Germans for over three years.

"They have fortified lines across the hill, and employed machine gun nests with interlocking fields of fire. The artillery will open their bombardment with a preparatory barrage. They will then commence a rolling barrage to destroy barbed wire and some machine gun nests in the enemy lines. You will assault the German lines with rifle fire, grenades, and Stokes 3 inch mortars.

"You must move rapidly, to cut off the German line of retreat. I expect you to hit them hard with each of your companies. I want this entire regiment to give good account of itself in the morning. This is why we are over here. We need to kill some German, and win this war.

"Keep the men spread out when we go over the top.

"Gentleman, allied aircraft have made over flights between here and Metz, and they have carefully taken reconnaissance of most of the machine gun nests between here and our objectives. They have cataloged each known machine gun nest onto a set of grid coordinates that have been fed to the artillery commanders, and they will proceed to bombard the German machine gun posts at 0420 hours tomorrow morning. The gun fire will continue for two full hours, and then we will be ordered to attack at 0630 hours.

"Hill Number 42 is located approximately three and one half miles west of the Moselle River. There are several German machine gun nests in and around Hill 42, and they must be taken or destroyed. The entire First Corps, consisting of the 2nd and 5th Divisions, and the 90th and 82nd Divisions will attack along our front. The 4th Corps will also attack along the salient along with the French 39th Division and French 26th Division. The entire French 26th Division will attack on both sides of the St. Mihiel salient. Our objective is to drive due north toward Metz. The French will be satisfied with simply recapturing the angle of the salient, but our commanders want us to drive hard toward the French railway junction near Metz.

"Each of you at this moment are being handed silver plated whistles by Sergeant Major Sims. At the time that the over the top command is issued, you are to blow the whistle loudly, and lead your company out the dugouts and across the no man's land in on the attack.

"Aerial reconnaissance and local intelligence has advised us that the Germans have cleared away brush, and have created interlocking fields of fire with their machine gun posts. Their defense mechanism appears to be a defense in depth. Unless the machine gun nests are officially knocked out, your causalities will be heavy. I anticipate that Allied artillery will knock out some of the machine gun nests, but the bulk of the machine gun nests must be destroyed by your men.

"Detail two men in each platoon with wire nippers to ensure that you will penetrate the German barb wire perimeter, and detail at least one mortar team per platoon to assist you in knocking out the machine gun nest that are located at near top of the hill. Let us synchronize our watches. It is now 1817 hours on my watch, mark.

"Do not advance you men through the shell craters created by high explosive shells. Go around the shell craters completely.

"I will issue follow up orders to you after we have assaulted Hill 42. Good luck, men. That is all. Go take our orders to you men. God grant us the power and the glory to take a victory on the morrow."

Stephen and Carl left the headquarters dugout, and trudged up the trench back to their company area. When Stephen got back to his command post, he had Sergeant Sanders spread the word about the morning attack.

Stephen went into his dugout and found his small chair and table, and removed his helmet, and sat down before his hurricane lamp to read the letter that Ned Sanders had sent him.

He began to read, and his joy at learning that Loralie had borne him a son became tainted by the horror of the news that Loralie had been unfaithful to him. He felt a sickening, stabbing pain in the pit of his stomach.

The paternity of his son was in question. He was totally devastated. While he was training to serve his country as an infantry officer, his wife was having carnal relations with another man. His anger overpowered him. He would deal with Loralie in divorce court once he returned to Royston. He would kill her lover, and throw his carcass off the top of Buzzard Knob. God help the Germans tomorrow as well.

He began to collect his thoughts a few moments later when Lieutenant Sam Turner entered his dugout.

"Sir, what shall I tell the men about the attack tomorrow?"

Stephen rubbed his face, and began to collect himself. He was an infantry captain in the United States Army. He was seething on the inside, but he had a job to do. He must attend to his duties.

"Lieutenant, tell them that a preparatory artillery bombardment will commence at 0420 hours. The shelling will abate at 0620 hours. We will go over the top at 0630 hours. Tell the men to have their gas masks, and equipment at the ready when the bombardment begins. We will attack the German emplacements on Hill 42. It will be up to us to knock out their machine gun nests, carry their works, and get into the German rear. Pass this word around to all of the NCOs in the company. Tell the men we are to spread out when we go over the top."

"Yes, sir."

Lieutenant Turner saluted Stephen, and walked back down to the main company dugout to tell the men.

Stephen felt ill. He stripped his uniform tunic, and put on an extra undershirt before replacing his tunic. He was cold in the chilly, damp French weather, but he was not going to wear his officer's trench coat.

He was going to carry his full equipment belt and his rifle, and he wanted no garment to get in the way of his access to his weapons and his equipment on his belt.

He went over to his wash basin and washed his face. He then

summoned First Sergeant Sanders.

"Carl, I want you to cut off one of the dog tags of each man that falls in battle tomorrow. You are to bring them to me. I will write letters home to their kin folks in the event that a soldier is killed in action. Don't tell the men about this, sergeant. Just let that be our secret."

"Yes, sir. Good night, sir."

"Good night. Tell the men to some rest."

Stephen turned down his hurricane lamp, and stretched out across his cot. He was angry and hurt, and could not get to sleep as soon as he would have liked. But sleep did come, in his damp dugout in Central France.

The next morning at 0420 hours, the American artillery opened up on the German lines. Hundreds of guns had been assembled with high explosive rounds, and at the signal of a single gun, all of the remaining batteries opened fire.

It seemed to Stephen that the heavens had opened up to rain thunder, fire and death on the Germans. He saw the yellow flames in the heavens, heard the crashes and booms of the 75 mm guns, and heard the whistling and screaming of the shells overhead.

The shells exploded in rolling thunder across the way into the German lines, tearing out barbed wire traps, and destroying German machine guns and bunkers on Hill 42.

Stephen tightened the chin strap on his helmet, and took out his pocket watch. He noted the time, 0504 hours.

He passed the word for First Lieutenant Turner. When Lt. Turner arrived, he was wearing his trench coat. "Lieutenant, pass the word among the NCOs that these shells from our guns are going to plow up dirt and make some craters. There are also some old craters out there that are full of mud and rainwater."

"The men will get bogged down and held up in those craters, and they will be easy marks for the German machine gunners."

"If possible, you are to go around the shell holes, do you understand?"

"Yes, sir. I understand, sir."

"Very well. Get your whistle ready and you will lead the second platoon over the top." See you on the hill."

"Thank you, sir."

Lieutenant Turner saluted Stephen, and went back down the dugout as the American bombardment continued. The German gunners did not answer with counter battery fire. Stephen figured that they were saving their shells for the attack that they knew would come on Hill 42.

Stephen sent for First Sergeant Carl Sanders.

"Yes, sir." Carl had his rifle in his hand, and was ready for the attack.

"Have two of the men with the wire cutters come with us when we go over the top. I want us to get through the barbed wire as quickly as we can."

"Yes, sir. A mortar crew will be right behind us as well."

"Very good. The gunfire will lift directly. Maybe some of these boys have blasted a big hole in the wire for us to run through."

"Wishful thinking sir?"

"Carl, do you have any extra hand grenades?"

"Yes, sir. You can take two of mine. Here you are, sir."

"Thank you. I'm sure that we will draw machine gun fire from the hill. We have got to flank them out of their positions when we get to their posts on the ridge line."

Carl looked over at Stephen, and noticed the worried look on his face.

"We'll do just fine sir. Those men have trained hard for this."

"You're right, First Sergeant. We need to get ready. The artillery fire will lift directly."

"Yes, sir."

The artillery fire did lift at 0620 hours, after the rolling barrage moved toward Hill 42. Stephen noticed a yellow streak over the horizon, and then a pink streak soon appeared in the eastern French sky.

He could soon make out the shapes of the soldiers in the trench,

93

and he took out his pocket watch and noted the time, 0626 hours.

He looked at his watch, and then at the small picture of Loralie, Millie and Annie on the inside corner of the pocket watch. The thought of Lori's infidelity sickened him again, and sent waves of anger into his heart.

He hoped that God would have mercy on the Germans that day, for he would give them none. The Germans caused him to go to war. They caused his wife to commit adultery on account of her loneliness. Now they would pay a price for what they had done. He would see to it.

He regained his composure, and took his place near the assault ladder at the trench. He pulled his Colt .45 pistol from its holster, slid the bolt back, and chambered a round into the chamber. He uncocked the weapon, locked on the safety, and slid it back into its holster.

He grabbed his rifle, and slung it over his shoulder. He reached around his neck, and grabbed a silver plated whistle which was hung on a chain. He put the whistle to his lips, and then took out his pocket watch. Two minutes later, at 6:30 a.m., he blew two long blasts on the whistle, and ordered "Over the top, men, advance forward!"

He climbed the ladder, and stepped out over the sandbags that lined the opposite side of the bunker.

He looked down the line, and saw hundreds of 82nd Division soldiers climbing out of the trenches, and advancing in the dim light of the French morning.

Company "I" had been detailed to assault the ridge line of Hill 42. Stephen saw several shell craters, and saw that a large gap had been blasted in the barbed wire by the rolling barrage. He dodged the shell craters, and pushed forward. He saw the jawbone of a mule, and part of an artillery harness half buried in the muck on the side of a shell crater.

He looked several hundred yards above him at the ridge line, and saw several thick strands of pine trees and English Oaks. He looked over the left, and saw a dead German machine gun crew. Smoke was wafting from their bloodied bodies, where a high explosive shell had killed them that morning.

He moved his men forward, and then began to move for the first stand of trees at the foot of Hill 42.

Two hundred yards up the ridge, the German machine gun bunkers then went into action. Stephen heard the cadence of their steady fire and noticed that it sounded like a typewriter. The German machine gunner fired away, as the U.S. soldiers came into range. Stephen saw four men go down at once.

He sprinted for an English Oak twenty yards ahead, and dove for its base, ducking for cover. A machine gun burst was fired just above his head, and he heard the thumps as the rounds struck the oak above him.

He chambered a .303 round into his Enfield rifle, and carefully peered at the gun crew.

They were 160 yards away. He waited until the gunner moved away at targets to his right on the ridge, and then he took aim and fired. The gunner pitched forward. He quickly chambered another .303 round and shot the second gunner as he took control of the weapon. The German ammo man began to move the second gunner out of the way, so he could work the weapon.

Stephen chambered another .303 round and shot the ammo man through the ear flap of his coal scuttle helmet.

Stephen then advanced from the English Oak, and moved his troops forward. He began to climb the ridge at an angle, with an eye toward the other German machine gun nest.

He waded through a small creek, and picked his way past some birch and alder trees, and then listened for the chattering of the second German machine gun.

He crept closer to the ridge along the cold water creek, when he heard the machine gun open up on more American soldiers.

He looked up the hill for another 200 yards and saw U.S. soldiers falling over backwards after being hit by the German machine gun fire.

He sprinted up the slope, over a ditch dug by the German scout troops, and up near the area where the machine gun was in action.

Stephen noticed that the men were all pinned down by the machine gun fire, around the base of the hill, hugging trees for cover. He saw Sergeant Sanders, and crawled to the oak tree where he was hiding from the gunfire.

"Carl, how many German soldiers are up there with the machine gun post?"

The machine gun fired at an area above them.

"About thirty-five, sir. Four men have been detailed to serve the gun. They have a cement bunker with a tin roof over it up there, sir."

Stephen got his small binoculars from his backpack, and began to survey the machine gun post. He knew what had to be done to conquer the position.

"Carl, get Corporal Cain up here with the Stokes mortar. There is a small trench about forty yards back of those trees that would make a good place to set up a firing position for the mortars. Tell Corporal Cain to put mortar fire on the tin roof of the machine gun post, and then on the soldiers' entrenchments.

Have Corporal Ford report to me with five men. I want to climb the ridge and put on a flanking fire."

Ten minutes later, Corporal Richard Ford reported to Stephen with five men from his second platoon. Stephen ordered them to follow him up the ridge, and they began to move back and forth between beech and hickory trees on the slope.

The machine gun then began to fire a burst in their direction. Stephen heard bullets thud and impact beech trees to his left. He also heard bullets smack into the flesh of Private Wayne Hamby, and he saw Private Hamby fall to the ground on his left.

Stephen and Corporal Ford sprinted to a large pine tree, where they had a view of the machine gun nest at a forty degree angle up the slope of the hill.

Stephen chambered a round into his Enfield .303, and took aim at the top of the gunner's helmet. He fired, and the gunner pitched forward. A second German soldier with a coal scuttle helmet began to work the gun, firing a burst at a group of the U.S. soldiers below their position.

Five men went down at once. Stephen then heard the bang of a shell as it was ejected from the Stokes mortar below them, and he then heard the incoming shell as it flew over to the machine gun post.

The shell exploded to the right of the German position, blowing up sandbags and severely wounding a couple of German soldiers.

Stephen fired another round at the machine gunner at 175 yards. The second gunner also pitched forward. A second Stokes mortar shell also came in, and it exploded just above the tin roof of the German dugout.

The German position was destroyed, as the shell killed five German soldiers when the bunker blew apart.

Stephen had his small squad advance on the positions, but only found dead and dying German soldiers there.

They continued their advance up the slope of Hill 42. With their packs and weapons and equipment, they zig zagged their way up through the pine and oak trees.

They soon came within sight of another line of entrenchments, which ran at right angles across the crown of the hill. The pine timber had been cleared for several yards in front of the trenches, to give the soldiers a wider field of fire.

Stephen took out his field glasses, and looked over the German position.

Two platoons of soldiers held the top of the hill. He also saw a traverse tunnel that disappeared into the top of Hill 42. A machine gun post was mounted on a concrete bunker close the entrance of the traverse tunnel.

Stephen sent for Lieutenant Sam Turner. He arrived a few minutes later, huffing and puffing from his climb above the slope.

"Sam, I want you to take two platoons of men and one mortar crew about three hundred yards north of their position. I will have the rest of the men assault those works from here.

"We want to take their entire position under fire from three different directions. You will attack once you hear us fire upon their position. I will wait for thirty minutes until you get into position. Do you understand my orders?"

"Yes, sir."

"Very well. Carry on, Lieutenant Turner. Good Luck."

"Thank you, sir."

Lieutenant Turner saluted, and began to assemble his men for the final assault on Hill 42. The Germans could barely see them as they began to creep around the outside of the tree line to their attack positions.

Stephen surveyed the German trenches with his binoculars. He then concluded that the Germans were not firing because they were ordered to conserve their ammunition. He took out his pocket watch, and noted the time, ten thirty.

He summoned First Sergeant Sanders, and began to issue orders to the remainder of his company through him.

"Carl, I want a mortar crew to place fire on the machine gun nest at the top of the hill. You will have them set up behind that English Oak down there, but out in the clearing. The Germans will take them under fire there, so you will need to send a squad of riflemen there to give them some cover.

"Have them get ready to attack this hill in twenty minutes. They will fire four or five rounds at the machine gun, and then put two more rounds into the German trenches. They will then break down their weapon, and advance forward with me. I will signal them to open fire when I fire off a single shot. Do you understand my orders?"

"Yes, sir. I will get them into position."

Carl left to get Corporal Vinson and his Stokes mortar crew into position.

Stephen walked over to the stump of a large English Oak, and laid his rifle across the stump.

Twenty minutes later, Sergeant Sanders reported back to him.

"Corporal Vinson and his crew are in position, sir."

"Thank you, First Sergeant."

Stephen looked down the slope at the men, who were laying down, but were all facing the enemy position. He saw rows of flat American metal helmets, interposed between the trees of the hill.

He took his Enfield .303 rifle, and aimed at the German machine gun nest. It was 200 yards away. He fired at the lead gunner, and the gunner fell back into the bunker. He then heard the flight of the mortar shells up the hill, and the whistling sound of air rushing past the shells as they fell. He then saw an explosion up on the machine gun bunker. Several separate explosions detonated around the concrete bunker, and Stephen saw bodies fly out the side of the machine gun nest.

Several shells also landed in the trenches, exploding there, and scattering German soldiers and sandbags like ten pins.

Stephen then stood up from his position, and blew his silver plated whistle, and shouted "FORWARD!"

At once, the American soldiers stood and advanced in a continuous line up the slope of Hill 42.

Once the U.S. soldiers emerged from the tree line, the German troops in gray uniforms and coal scuttle helmets began to pour rifle fire into them.

Stephen closed to within a hundred yards of the German line when he heard more bullets whiz past his helmet. He then saw several more German soldiers emerge from the blasted entrance of the tunnel wearing funny looking tanks on their backs.

As Lieutenant Turner's platoon closed near the German dugout, Stephen saw several American soldiers fall to the ground after being shot. He then saw a flash of fire, and a stream of chemical flame shoot out from the German works.

Several U. S. soldiers were set fully on fire. Some men began screaming and turning as they burned; other men died almost instantly, and fell face forward.

Stephen dropped to one knee, and took aim at the flame throwing tank of a German storm trooper. He fired, and the tank exploded, spreading flames and death among the German troops in the trenches.

He stopped and shouted at Sergeant Sanders: "Shoot their tanks! Order the men to shoot their flame throwing tanks!"

Carl dropped to one knee aimed at another storm trooper, and fired his .303 Enfield. The trooper's tank also exploded, causing chaos and confusion within the German works.

Stephen began to run, dodging a U.S. corporal who was shot in the face in front of him. He stopped twenty yards from the trenches, and began to aim and fire at German soldiers until he had emptied his Enfield magazine.

He drew his Colt .45 pistol, and ran toward the German dugout. He saw a German officer reach for his pistol, but Stephen fired, and the shot knocked the officer off his feet at 30 yards. Other soldiers from the 82nd Division closed the gap, and they all assaulted the German line at its salient point.

Stephen shot and killed five more German soldiers with his pistol, but the Government Colt then jammed. A big German private lunged at him with the fixed bayonet on his Mauser rifle.

Stephen stepped to one side on the edge of the trench, and grabbed a shovel that was lodged behind a sandbag.

He quickly blocked the German's bayonet with the shovel, and then expertly brought the shovel up, slashing hard at an angle to his left.

He caught the German in the throat, severing his carotid artery. He saw the German soldier fall over, clutching at his bloody throat, and he then looked up and around his position.

Lieutenant Turner and his entire platoon had captured the German fortification, and German officers and men were ordered to walk out of the woods with their hands on their heads.

Stephen looked over from the trench, and saw the smoldering remains of one of his history students, twenty year old Walter Johnson, just a few feet away.

Stephen became enraged when he thought of the horrible deaths that his men had suffered at the flame throwing hands of the storm troopers.

He reached down, and pulled the bolt back on his Government Colt, engaging it.

He aimed at the last remaining storm trooper and fired, placing one round in his head and another round in his chest.

Lieutenant Turner took offense. "But sir, these men have surrendered. We can't shoot them like this."

Stephen holstered the pistol. "Lieutenant, I can and *will* shoot the sons of bitches that burn my boys alive. Look over there at one of your classmates. See him over there, that was Walter Johnson. I will not tolerate an enemy that burns men alive like dogs. If the enemy engages in this conduct again, I and I alone on this field will determine who lives and who dies when we carry a German position.

"Only animals burn men to death like that. If anyone in your outfit speaks any German, tell these men that I will give no quarter to any German soldier that burns my men. Lieutenant, send for Corporal Evans. I need him now."

"Yes, sir."

Stephen removed his helmet, sat down on a sandbag, and began to write a note to Colonel Charles Harker that he would send by carrier pigeon:

September 13, 1918
Colonel Charles Harker
325th Infantry Division HQ

Colonel:

We have carried Hill No. 42. We will herd the prisoners to the rear, and will push on to Boullionville tonight.

Captain Stephen Harris
Commanding Co. I

Stephen gave the message to Corporal Daniel Evans of the Signal Corps, and then sent for First Sergeant Sanders.

"Carl, report our casualties, if you will."

"Twenty dead, five burned to death, sir. Fifteen wounded. Four are critical, sir."

"Give me one of the dog tags of each of the dead, Carl. I will write their mothers and send home a single dog tag from each soldier. The burial parties will need the other dog tag to identify their bodies later. Get the wounded back to the aid station. We will push on to Boullionville in three hours."

"Yes, sir. Right away, sir."

Stephen reached into his haversack, and took out a piece of hardtack, and a piece of hard cheese. He pulled out his canteen, and took his water, and ate his cold rations in silence. He could remember each of the names and the faces of the boys that fell today. He then pulled his canteen back into place on his belt, and began to get ready for the final push into Boullionville.

CHAPTER ELEVEN

August 19, 1918
Captain Stephen Harris
Co. "I," 325th Infantry Rgmnt
APO AEF
France

Darling:

I have good news for you! Four days ago, I gave birth to a beautiful eight and half pound son. He has dark hair and blue eyes, and big hands, just like you. We had previously discussed his name, darling, and I named him Matthew Clayton Harris. Matthew was my Grandpa's name, and Clayton was your father's middle name. This was what we had agreed to name him before you left for France. I hope you are doing fine, and remain in good spirits. I hope and pray that you and your men will finish this war up soon, so you can return home to me.

Tell Carl that Sheila has been a Godsend to us. Even though she is expecting a child of her own, she has cooked food for me and the girls, and she has cleaned and done work for me while I was bedridden. Your son is beautiful, healthy, and stays hungry for my breasts.

I am fine, darling, and will be back on my feet real soon. I asked Ned to post this letter for me when he goes into Carnesville with his milk run. I hope and pray for your safe return, and the resumption of our life together, love. Until I see you again, I am your loving wife.

Loralie

P.S. Annie and Millie send their love to you as well.

Loralie looked over at the crib where Matthew was sleeping, and then folded the letter carefully and placed it into an envelope. She sealed the envelope and addressed it at Stephen's desk in the study, and put postage on the envelope as well.

The next Sunday was homecoming at the New Pentecostal Church. There would be a sermon and a dinner on the grounds, and her Uncle Jack had invited her family several weeks ago to the homecoming sermon and dinner. Ned Sanders had agreed to drive them that morning, and Sheila was also going to attend services with them.

Loralie had begun to experience guilty feelings about her affair with Mark Lake. He was deeply infatuated with her. He was an attentive and caring lover and companion, but he was young, and he was not her husband.

Annie and Millie would not accept him if she were to acknowledge Mark openly. Ned Sanders certainly would not accept her relationship with him. Mark had met her companionship and sexual needs, but she did not really love him.

Their relationship was illicit in every way. If Stephen survived the war, she must break off her relationship with Mark, and make him understand why. She felt no immediate need to confess her adultery to Stephen, though. If he had not left her and the girls, she would not have been unfaithful. She felt no guilt about her conduct, by justifying her actions as she did.

She sat at her dresser and rolled up her hair, hoping she might catch a glimpse of Mark Lake at the church dinner. He had been attending church services for the past four months, so he could see her on Sundays. He was in love with her, and wanted all of her, not just the part of her life she had given him.

She pinned on her straw hat, and checked the front of her dress. Sheila had made her some dresses with buttons on the sides of her breast, which would allow her to nurse the baby more easily.

The baby had to eat, even at the church services. Annie ran into her room in her navy blue dress and informed her that Ned and Sheila were outside.

She got up her bag, and told Millie to get their lunch basket. She had fried some chickens that Millie had killed the day before, and she had prepared sandwiches and deviled eggs for their dinner as well.

She reached into the crib and got the sleeping baby, and they soon loaded up into Ned Sander's GMC truck. The girls sat on blankets back of the cab, and Loralie and the baby sat in the cab with Sheila and Ned.

Twenty five minutes later in the morning heat, the GMC truck pulled into a small field adjacent to a small white clapboard church.

Two small boys in overalls were pulling on a rope that rang the church bell in the steeple. Annie and Millie, dressed in navy blue dresses and lace up boots, brought their lunch over to a large table behind the church which was filled with food.

Ladies in aprons and straw hats could be seen walking about the table, putting the food for the dinner in some sort of order.

Little girls with fans swatted at the flies. The table was under a long tin roof, which provided shade from the summer sun, but no type of relief for the heat and the flies.

After Annie and Millie dropped off the food, the family filed into the church, where the usher seated them conveniently on a back row pew.

Pastor Amos Alexander was already at the podium, wearing a black frock coat, and a black bow tie. He welcomed the regular members and visitors alike to the homecoming services and dinner, and asked the music minister to lead the congregation in song.

A young man in a brown shirt and black trousers began to direct them to turn in their hymnals to page 354, and to sing the first, second, and last verse of "Amazing Grace." He asked the congregation to stand while singing.

The church members opened their hymnals, and stood together to sing. Loralie remained seated with little Clayton. Halfway through the song, Clayton woke up, and he began to cry and fuss. He was hungry.

Loralie excused herself, grabbed her small bag, and filed out of the church. She walked to a bench located under a Blackjack Oak behind the privy.

She sat down and unbuttoned her dress, and gave Clayton the nipple of her left breast to suckle. She covered herself with a shawl she had brought for that purpose, and began to enjoy the quiet moment away from the church while Clayton nursed.

Eighteen minutes later, Clayton fell asleep at her breast, so she wiped off his mouth with a rag, and carried him inside the sanctuary.

Sheila had been begging Loralie to let her hold the baby, and Loralie gladly handed the sleeping infant over to her.

Pastor Amos Alexander had begun his message, and he was reading from the book of Numbers, Chapter 32, verse 23.

"But if ye will not do so, behold, ye have sinned against the Lord; and be sure your sin will find you out." He then asked the congregation to turn to the book of Revelation, Chapter 18, verses 3 and 5: "for all nations have drunk the wine of the wrath of her fornication, and the kings of the earth have committed fornication with her and the merchants of the earth are waxed such through the abundance of her delicacies ... For her sins have reached into heaven, and God hath remembered her iniquities."

"Let us pray: Our precious heavenly father, let thy word bring conviction on those hearts it is meant to reach. Let the seed of thy word be sewn in rich, good earth and take root. Use me as thy servant to bring thy word to the hearts of those that must be convicted of their sin, so the blood of thy Lamb can cleanse them of their sins, we ask in Jesus name, Amen."

Pastor Alexander then spoke of God's love, and spoke of sin being a gulf between God and man, and how Jesus of Nazareth, Jesus Christ, was sent by God to wash away the sins of the world.

He began to quote scriptures from his memory. "And it says that in Romans, Chapter 10, that it is written that of them shalt confess with thy mouth to the Lord Jesus, and shalt believe in thine heart that God hath raised him from the dead, thou shalt be saved.

"For with the heart man believeth unto righteousness; and with the mouth confession is made unto salvation."

Every word that came from Brother Amos' mouth seemed to be

directed at Loralie, she believed. She had felt no substantial guilt about her adulterous affair with Mark Lake, up until now.

She then heard Pastor Alexander plead his case a final time, as he stepped down from the pulpit and out in front of the altar:

"Have you any unfinished business with Jesus Christ today? All you have to do is stand up and walk down here when we play an invitation, and stand here beside me. You then ask Jesus Christ to forgive you of your sin, acknowledge your sin to him, and you will be saved. This is how it is written in the book of Romans, your confession will be made into your salvation. If sin is in your heart, and if the Holy Spirit has convicted you, you come. Brother, please now give the Hymn of Invitation."

The young man in the brown shirt and black tie asked the congregation to stand and sing hymn of Invitation No. 302, "Just as I Am." The congregation began to sing.

Loralie did not know what had come over her. She put her hymnal down into a rack in the pew in front of her, and slowly stood to her feet. She stepped out into the aisle, not knowing how her feet could be moving her forward. She walked down the aisle to the altar, and knelt down beside Brother Amos. She had been fully and completely convicted of her sin, and as she knelt with her head down, the tears began to pour down her cheeks.

CHAPTER TWELVE

The following morning, Stephen and his company were on the outskirts of Boullionville. He had made his headquarters in a bombed out old windmill, where he ate his canned ration, and brewed himself some coffee on a small spirit stove in the mill.

He was putting on his helmet, when First Sergeant Sanders reported in.

"Sir, we have an officer coming in on horseback. He's dressed a little funny, but I believe he's a bird colonel, sir."

"I'll come out and greet him, and see if he has any orders for us."

"He's coming up from the other side of Boullionville, sir."

"Very, well, let's see what's on his mind."

Stephen walked through the open door of the old windmill, and saluted the colonel as he dismounted his white horse.

Corporal Ford held the horses's bridle while the officer dismounted. He was dressed in a thick trench coat, and a felt officer's cap, and he carried no side arms. He only had a funny little riding crop with him, if you could call that a weapon, Stephen thought.

Stephen saluted the colonel, and the NCOs then did likewise.

The colonel returned his salute, and began to ask questions.

"Captain, what outfit is this?"

"Company I, 325th Infantry Regiment, sir. I'm in command. Captain Stephen Harris, sir."

"And where have you advanced over the past day and half?"

"We captured Hill 42, sir, and have pushed on to this point."

"I heard about your work up there, Captain. Your 82nd Division will put you in for the Silver Star for what you did up there. What intelligence can you give me of the enemy's movements?"

"Sir, we have encountered no German artillery. I have seen the trenches left behind by their soldiers. We found no 88 mm ammunition or guns in any position when we overran this sector. It appears, sir, that they have withdrawn all of their artillery from this sector. We have encountered some stiff resistance, but it's mostly rear guard troops they have left behind. Their main defenses have obviously been relocated elsewhere."

"I see. Captain, I have been all the way beyond Boullionville, and have even looked into Metz. I am going to recommend a heavy attack in this sector, based on your information, and the information I have obtained from this scouting excursion. What is your analysis of the situation here?"

"Colonel, we should exploit this withdrawal the fullest. We may never be presented a better opportunity to pierce the Hindenberg line at such a lightly defended point. Remember what Longstreet's Corps did at Chickamauga, sir."

"You sound like a West Point man, Captain."

"No, sir. I have a B.A. in history from the University of Georgia, sir. I was a history professor at Franklin County High School before the war, sir."

"You keep reminding us of our history, captain. It does teach us lessons we all need to remember while we fight this war. Carry on, and keep up the good work."

"Thank you , sir. Colonel? I never got your name, sir."

The Colonel pulled the reins around on his horse, and the horse turned back to the sandy road.

"It's MacArthur. Colonel Douglas MacArthur. Carry on, Captain."

"Yes, sir."

Stephen saluted the colonel, as he rode his mount back along the sandy road away from Boullionville.

Carl was impressed. "That was Colonel MacArthur. He has a lot of influence with Black Jack Pershing. He said they put you in for a Silver Star, sir, what an honor!"

Stephen was also impressed. "We need to march on through Boullionville. Tell the men to fall in behind those two tanks that are advancing on the town. Their machine guns will give us some covering fire if we get attacked on the street."

"Yes, sir. We all will be leaving here directly then, sir?"

"That's right, Carl. Get a bugler with a whistle to sound the advance. We are going to take the town."

They advanced through a peach orchard, when they came under fire from a German machine gun. Stephen heard the cadence of the gun, and saw men falling back on the other side of the orchard. He waved his arms, and signaled the company to spread out. The peach trees were in full canopy, so they offered concealment at a distance from the machine gun nest.

He sent for Lieutenant Turner, and a mortar crew from his platoon. The Stokes mortar and the ammunition were brought up in ten minutes.

"Lieutenant Turner, have the crew lob two rounds at about 120 yards over to the opposite side of the orchard."

"Yes, sir."

The Stokes mortar was sighted toward the sound of the machine gun, and a round was loaded into the tube.

The round was thrown up and out above the trees, and it exploded a hundred yards away. The explosion uprooted a peach tree, and threw up a small cloud of smoke. The machine gun commenced firing, a sign that the round had missed.

Lieutenant Turner barked his orders to the mortar crew. "Elevate ten degrees, and aim to the right at ten o'clock."

The crew obeyed, and fired a second round, which exploded closer to the edge of the orchard. Lieutenant Turner observed the explosion with his field glasses, and issued another order.

"Fire two more rounds for effect."

The mortar rounds exploded over the German position, but one of the machine guns continued to fire at them.

Stephen issued orders to First Sergeant Sanders to assault the German machine gun nest, when an American light tank rumbled through the orchard, and began to engage the German positions.

The tank raked the Germans with machine gun fire, killing all of the gunners and their ammo men as well.

Stephen ordered an advance, when Sergeant Sanders brought a dispatch from Corporal Evans of the Signal Corps. "This just came in from carrier pigeon, sir. It is an order from Colonel Harker, sir."

September 15, 1918
Captain Stephen Harris
Co. I, 325th Infantry Regiment

Captain:
   You are hereby ordered to halt your advance, and to return to your original lines of September 12th. The regiment will reform there, to countermarch north by west, to the Argonne Sector.
   This is by order of Generals Pershing and Foch.

Respectfully,

Charles Harker
Commanding 325th Infantry

   Stephen despised the order. There would be no better opportunity to breach the Hindenberg line with such little cost in casualties than the present.
   General Foch and General Pershing did not realize that the Germans had partially pulled out of the St. Mihiel sector. This gave the American Army a grand opportunity. Only the stupidity of higher command stood in the way of their opportunity to breach the German main defenses.
   Metz was theirs for the taking, but orders were orders. Stephen knew that they must be obeyed.
   "First Sergeant Sanders, send for a bugler. Halt the advance. Sound the recall. We have been ordered to another sector."
   "Why, sir, Why now? We could roll these Germans up like a blanket now, sir. Why are they recalling us?"
   Stephen was angry about many things, and his frustration bubbled to the surface.
   "The French and the British don't want us to break through and win this war, Carl. They think that if we beat the Germans ourselves,

that we will win the right to dictate peace based on the Fourteen Points. They recalled us because they don't want us to totally break the German defenses on our own.

"General Foch gave the order, I am sure. What I can't stomach is the fact that General Pershing forgets he is an American general first, and an Allied general second. We had our own reasons for getting into this war. We should have been turned loose to finish it."

"Now, we have to go back. Sound the recall, bugler, then sound assembly. Come on, Carl, we have to go back."

"Yes, sir. I understand, sir"

The bugler sounded the recall, and then sounded "assembly." Stephen issued written orders to all the NCOs to march the men back to their original jump off point below Hill 42. They soon broke down their gear, and they began to slog back to their lines where they started on September 12th.

Colonel George C. Marshall of General Pershing's staff was given the job of ordering the U.S. First Army to countermarch from the St. Mihiel Sector over to new positions in the Argonne Forest.

It was the greatest logistical feat of the war. Thousands of men, mules, weapons, tanks, guns and equipment had to be moved over muddy roads to their new position in a matter of days.

The muddy French roads soon became clogged with weapons, guns, and tanks. Stephen's Company "I," after marching northwest all night, soon encountered a stalled column of 75 mm guns in the road. The stalled guns had created a huge traffic jam, and Stephen ordered the men to file up to the front of the column to see what could be done about the situation.

They squeezed to the front of the column, to see a 75 mm gun stuck up to its axles in the black French mud. A big burly sergeant was whipping his mule across the rump with a pair of Army suspenders, but the gun just would not move.

Stephen saw the situation, and pitched in at once. "Let me help you, Sergeant. Men, grab the mule's harness and push forward, on my command. Heave! Heave! Heave!"

The men began to push on the rear of the stuck wheels of the gun carriage, and the gun began to move forward slowly. The mud soon yielded up the carriage wheels with a sucking sound, and the mules pulled the gun free, and up the road. The men cheered, and the column began to move again.

The skies cleared off, and Stephen noticed a flight of Allied biplanes overhead. They waggled their wings as they flew over the slogging columns of infantry and artillerymen. The artillery sergeant came over and shook Stephen's hand.

"Fly boys in airplanes don't have to worry about the mud sir, but we sure do. Thank you for your help. I'm sure our captain would have appreciated it as well."

Stephen asked the sergeant who is captain was .

"Captain Harry S. Truman, sir, from Battery D, 129th Regiment. He's gone ahead to the front of the column, sir. But I'll tell him you did us a favor."

"Tell him that Captain Stephen Harris from the 325th Infantry , 82nd Division paid you a visit, and I'll buy him a cup of coffee in Metz one day if he'll come see us."

"I will, sir. Thank you again, sir."

Stephen and his men slogged back to their company, and rejoined the march to the Argonne Forest. After a couple of hours, Stephen hitched a ride on an ammunition wagon. He had promised Sergeant Sanders that he would write home to the wives and mothers of the men that had died with Company "I" at Hill 42.

He pulled the dog tags of the fallen men from his backpack, as the ammunition wagon lurched forward. What could he tell the wives and mothers of those that had died up on Hill 42? What could he possibly say?

He pondered those things in his heart, and then he looked up to see the regimental color bearers march past his wagon, and up the road.

He saw the colors of the 325th Regiment, and the Stars and Stripes with 48 stars in a blue field, and tears came to his eyes.

He knew then what he would say, and he began to write with his pencil the first of many letters for his fallen men:

Headquarters on the March
Co. I, 325th Regiment
September 19, 1918

Mrs. Henry Morgan
RFD 4
Royston, Georgia

Dear Mrs. Morgan:
It is with great regret that I must inform you that your son, PFC. Thomas Morgan, was killed in action near Hill 42 on September 12th.

Thomas was a fine soldier, and he discharged his duties faithfully under my command. He died under fire while attacking a fortified German position.

While I cannot say or do anything that might justify your son's sacrifice, please accept my condolences for your loss. Your son died defending his country, the greatest republic on earth, and he died to end all wars. He was called to serve by our President, and to defeat a desperate foe in the name of freedom.

Your son died that so our nation might live, and his sacrifice shall not be in vain. We will win this war, and justify the cause for which Thomas gave his full devotion.

Enclosed is his dog tag that I have saved for you. I humbly request that you keep all of us in your prayers, as I pray for you now.

Respectfully yours,

Stephen Harris
Capt. Commanding Co. I
325th Infantry

As he folded and sealed the first of many letters, Stephen wiped a tear from his eye, and stuck his head out of the covered wagon. He called for Sergeant Sanders, who walked up to the rear of the moving wagon to give his report.

"Give me our total casualties from the other day, First Sergeant, if you will."

"Fourteen dead, twenty nine wounded, sir. Two of the wounded I believe are critical, sir. They are on ambulances now, sir, heading up to an aid station ahead. Sergeant Mudd was killed sir, from the second platoon."

"He was a good man, Have Corporal Fish take over for him. I should be done with these letters for home at the end of the day. Find us an Advanced Post Office wagon, so we can post them, if you will."

"I will see to that, sir. I'll let you get back to it, sir."

Sergeant Sanders saluted Stephen, and went up the road to find a mail wagon that would accept Stephen's letters for posting back to the U.S. While the ammon wagon continued up the muddy road, Stephen sharpened his pencil with his pen knife, and began another letter after pulling another dog tag from his backpack.

He knew all of those boys, because he had taught them all in school. He had once written their parents about their course progress in American and World History. Now he was writing their parents to inform them of their deaths. War is a horrible business, he thought, as he began to write his second letter for a fallen Doughboy.

Loralie had confessed her adultery and her infidelity to Brother Amos Alexander, who advised her to write to her husband, and to confess her sin to him, and attempt to seek his forgiveness.

On a warm and quiet summer evening, she sat down and composed a letter to Stephen, writing on the porch in the red splendor of the sunset. She choose her words carefully, but she knew it was time to confess her adultery, and to seek forgiveness from her husband.

September 12, 1918
Capt. Stephen Harris
Co. I, 325th Infantry Regiment
APO AEF
France

Dear Stephen:

I have something that I must tell you, love. I have broken the Seventh Commandment, and have committed adultery with a young railroad engineer after you joined the Army. I do not love him, but he was a charming man, and I was lonely. I have confessed my sin to the Lord, and have asked His forgiveness through the church.

Now I am writing you to confess my sins, and I can only tell you that I am truly sorry, and I now seek your pardon and your forgiveness. You are the one true love of my life, and I have jeopardized our family with my scandalous behavior. Please search deep into your kind and understanding heart, and tell me that you forgive me.

I want you, love. Only you. I miss you, and can only hope and pray that God will return you home to me safe and sound from this terrible war. If on the other hand, you return home and decide that you want to divorce me, I will understand. I am hoping and praying that you will find it in you heart to forgive me, and give me one more chance to regain happiness with the rest of our family. The girls and little Clayton are fine, and await your safe return from the war.

Until I hear from you, love, I am your loving wife,

Loralie

She sealed her letter, addressed the envelope, and left it out for Ned to post the following day when he would drive the girls to school.

She heard Clayton cry in the crib in the parlor, and she stepped inside to pick him up. She walked with him back to the porch and sat in her rocking chair, and began to unbutton her dress.

He began to nurse, and she leaned back in her rocker and watched the sunset glow red and orange over Buzzard Knob. His steady sucking on her breast made her feel peaceful, and at ease. She then wondered if Stephen would forgive her, or if he would ever survive the war.

CHAPTER THIRTEEN

Some 600,000 American troops were jamming the roads, moving to their attack positions in the Argonne Sector. Fifteen divisions of men, 3,000 pieces of artillery, tanks, trucks, and supply wagons continued to jam the roads leading to the new front.

The officers cursed the men and horses as they slogged forward in the mud, and straggling was strictly forbidden. Some of the officers drew their side arms to keep their men moving forward, as day ran into night.

The muddy march to the new front lasted an entire week. The length of the march was almost 100 miles, but each division arrived at its jump-off point on time.

The 82nd Division was soon ordered off the Bar-le-Duc Road, and into its position near the flank of the 28th Division at Varennes.

They arrived at their jump-off point in darkness at 4:00 a.m., and spent the next three days in preparation for "H-Hour," or their time of attack.

Trenches were dug and trees were cleared away from the front, and ammunition was hauled up. Stephen and the company officers were summoned on the second day to Colonel Harker's headquarters where some of the divisional officers from the 82nd were set up with a large map of the sector for a briefing.

Stephen took Carl with him to the briefing, and they filed into rows of folding wooden chairs and wooden cracker boxes that were set up before a crude platform. Lieutenant Turner came in late, clutching a small notebook and a pencil. Colonel Harker stood up and turned the meeting over to a Major Clark Mitchell, a red haired, freckle faced young officer with a crisply pressed staff uniform.

Major Mitchell worked on General Pershing's staff, and was briefing several of the Division commands that day. He strode to the podium, and began flipping pages in a notebook.

"Gentleman, this attack will be the single largest attack of this war. All Allied artillery, from Belgium on the English Channel, to

119

the French lines above Switzerland, will open fire on the enemy at once. The planned barrage will last several hours. Aeroplanes from the Allied sector will machine gun and bomb German positions just before the attack.

"Your attack will be on the flank of the 28th Division. You will have tanks to help you blast your way through barbed wire enclosures.

"Aerial reconnaissance has located several German machine gun bunkers in the immediate area on our front. The Germans are dug in on a large hogback, which is heavily wooded, and they have had three years to fortify their position. You must take them one hill at a time. The Allies need your courage, your dash, and your ability. Now it is time for you to step up and win the war.

"If we can push the Germans back across the Meuse, they will sue for peace. Our batteries will commence their bombardment with Mustard Gas shells. You will don your gas masks, and keep them on for at least 24 hours after the initial bombardment. The gas shells will be fired at 0420 hours on the morning of the 26th. The rolling barrage will commence at 0530 hours. You will attack with the entire First, Fifth and Third Corps at 0820 hours. I repeat, gentleman, 'H-Hour' will be at 0530 hours tomorrow morning. Good luck and God speed."

Major Mitchell stepped down from the podium, and was replaced by Colonel Harker, who answered some general questions, and then concluded the briefing.

Colonel Harker made his way over to Stephen as he was filing out of the briefing.

"Stephen, that was great work you did up on Hill 42. Division has awarded you the Silver Star. Division will award it to you next week. I have also nominated you for promotion to the rank of major. Your oak leaves should also come to you next week as well. I could use ten more officers like you, Stephen. It would make my work a whole hell of a lot easier."

"Thank you for the vote of confidence, sir. I'll do my best to not disappoint you."

"I know you won't. Next week, you will be in command of an

entire battalion of troops. Let me be the first to congratulate you, Stephen. I have sent Major Mabry over to brief your company on our attack orders.

"You may want to take this time to write a quick letter home. I'll see that it goes out with my correspondence. The Advanced Post Office has finally caught up with us."

"Thank you kindly, sir. I'll do that right now." Stephen saluted Colonel Harker, and then began to compose a quick letter back to Ned Sanders. He used a cracker box for a table, and he borrowed an inkwell and pen from Colonel Harker:

September 24, 1918
Near Varennes, France

Mr. Ned Sanders
RFD 1 Box 224
Royston Georgia

Dear Ned:

I am in receipt of your recent letter which announced the birth of my son, and which informed me that Loralie has been unfaithful to me. I know that letter was difficult for you to compose and sent to me, but I appreciate the candor and honesty of that act more than you will ever know.

We are now in the middle of the war. We are about to launch an attack on the Germans that will win this war. We have seen fighting a plenty already, and I have killed several German soldiers.

I have been too angry with Loralie to write her, and have been too busy with my duties to figure out how I might deal with her. I do know this, I have always wanted a son. If I survive the war, and return home, I will raise that boy as mine even if he actually isn't my natural son. Let that be our little secret. My marriage to Loralie may or may not survive, but to the entire world, I shall be Clayton's father in name and in deed.

We scored a major breakthrough in the St. Mihiel sector. If General Pershing would have let us, we would have advanced and pierced the Hindenberg Line, and the war would already be concluded by our forces.

Someone forgot to tell General Pershing that he is an American general first and an Allied general second. We had our own reasons for getting into this war. No so called ally should hold us back from defeating Germany. We need to push into Germany and totally destroy the Kaiser's war machine for all time, or little Clayton may be back over here fighting when he is grown. Enough of my soap box preaching.

This may be the last letter you ever get from me. Please send my love home to Annie, Millie, and little Clayton. Please tell Sheila that Carl is doing fine. I hope and pray that he survives this deadly war, and returns home to Royston. I have always loved you as my own father, and I hope that the next time I hear from you, your letter will bring nothing but good news. Loralie despised me for entering the service, but nothing I have ever done in this life is as important as what I have done here in France. If we do our work properly, there will be no need to send any more men from American to die on the fields of Europe.

Please hold down the fort for me at home.

Sincerely yours,

Stephen

Stephen addressed an envelope, sealed the letter inside, and found Colonel Harker's aid-de-camp, a Captain Griggers, who told him the letter would be sent for home on the next truck back to Paris.

He stopped a moment to look at the map, and the formidable German defenses located in their front. He believed deeply that the Germans had depleted their defenses in the St. Mihiel sector to beef up their defenses in the Ardennes.

If his hunch was correct, they would be attacking into the teeth of the prepared German defenses.

He walked back to the Company "I" assembly area, where he held an officer's call with the NCOs and Sergeant Sanders, and the lieutenants commanding the platoons. The officers and NCOs were briefed in detail about the attack orders, and every man present knew their orders by the close of the officer's call.

Stephen wrote out orders to Carl to bring up more ammunition for the men and the mortar crews. He sat down in his folding chair in his makeshift office in the dugout, and began to brew himself a small pot of tea on his spirit stove.

He soon had a steaming tin cup of tea in his hand, and he relaxed and enjoyed its warmth in the cool, dreary weather.

He had been incredibly angry at Loralie and her paramour, whoever he was. He was also angry at the Germans for killing some of his men horribly with fire.

His anger, though, was a controlled anger. It was anger with a purpose. He was not going to break. He had complete control of his faculties. He was channeling his anger and his fury at the Germans, now. Loralie would get it later, if he could get back to Royston.

He was going to do everything in his power to destroy any organized German force he contacted. He could not directly deal with this wife's infidelity just now, but he could kill some Germans. That was what he had trained to do.

He and his men were nothing more than killing machines. It was just a matter of how far they would be allowed to go. His goal was to break the Hindenberg Line, and invade Germany itself. Stephen wanted Kaiser Wilhelm tried as a war criminal.

He pulled up his cot, and removed his boots and helmet. He began to sleep soundly, as an eerie quiet fell over the front before them.

The bombardment began in the early morning chill of September 26th. 2700 Allied guns opened fire at once all along the Western front.

Stephen looked out at the horizon, and thought that part of the sky had caught fire.

The rolling barrage began at 0530 hours, and the shells began landing in a pattern away from the Allied lines, and out through the German defenses.

After the rolling barrage had lifted, Stephen donned his gas mask, and ordered all soldiers in Company "I" to do the same. At 0800 hours, Stephen moved to the ladder at the end of the trench, and checked his pocket watch.

He grabbed his canteen, lifted his mask, and took a long gulp of water. At 0829 hours, he lifted his mask, and placed his whistle to his lips. One minute later, he blew his silver plated whistle, re-donned his mask, and went over the top with his men.

The rolling barrage had destroyed the barbed wire defenses in their immediate front.

A light American tank soon came into view, and Stephen ordered the men to fall in and march behind it.

The tank smashed strands of barbed wire, and rolled around most the shell craters.

Stephen soon saw dead and dismembered German troops in small machine gun bunkers. They advanced steadily, taking only occasional small arms fire from German positions. Small American patrols at times would surround the German positions, and kill or capture all of the defenders.

26,000 American troops from ten different divisions began the attack, and the Germans simply could not deal with the weight in numbers. The German troops were killed, captured, and were forced back.

The further the Americans penetrated, the more that Stephen began to believe that the Germans had beefed up their defenses in the sector. He believed that the German defense philosophy had shifted to a defense in depth. If that was the case, then the best prepared defenses would be encountered later, at the top of the hill.

Just north of the town of Varennes, Stephen's Company "I" encountered two German machine gun nests in a large brick building that was partially standing.

A light tank was in the area, and Stephen ran down the tank, and tapped on its body. A Sergeant Masters poked his head through a gun hatch to speak to Stephen.

Stephen ordered the tank crew to support the infantry, and the tank advanced on the enemy machine gun posts.

The tank commander was Sergeant Frank Masters, who Stephen knew as a University of Georgia classmate.

The tank blasted the walls of the building with its gun, and the American soldiers shot the German crews as they exited the building.

A German plane began to dive in toward their position a few moments later, and the crewman in the rear seat began lobbing potato masher hand grenades their way. Several explosions detonated near their position.

Stephen ran into the bombed out building, and emerged with a German machine gun. He mounted it on top of a broken brick wall, and pulled the bolt back, and pointed the gun at the sky.

As the German Fokker flew by them, Stephen carefully led the plane, and began to fire machine gun bursts at the plane. He saw several shots hit the rudder and the fuselage, and the plane turned away from their position.

They pushed on past the town of Varennes, and toward the Aire River. Stephen received orders from Colonel Harker to push on, and push on he did.

The Germans were soon pushed back another five miles, and two days later, they were pushed back into their prepared defenses on the hilly acres of the Argonne Forrest. They had 77 mm artillery support on the tops of the hills, and the hills themselves were heavily wooded. Any ditches or ravines located on the hills had been dug deeper to discourage tank attacks from the Allied front.

On October 2, Stephen received new orders via an Army Signal Corps messenger pigeon. Stephen, unlike most officers, did not use telephone line communications, because the phone lines always got cut on the battlefield.

He took the message from Corporal Evans, and read it silently:

October 2, 1918
Headquarters near Baulny

Capt. Stephen Harris
Co. "I" 325th Regiment

Captain:

The regiment has been ordered off the present line, to march around and attack behind Apremont north to Farm des Granges. Your are to march to Baulny at once.

You will issue the appropriate marching orders to your men immediately.

Charles Harker
Colonel Commanding
325th Regiment

Stephen sent for Sergeant Sanders, and had him issue the recall order to the entire company. One hour later, the entire company began to march back through the battlefield north past the town of Apremont, and over to Baulny.

They saw dead horses and mules, and dead and wounded German and American soldiers along the way. They soon marched past a line of gassed and blinded American soldiers on their way to an aid station.

The blinded soldiers wore cloth blindfolds, and walked in a single file. Each soldier had his arm on the back of the soldier in front of him. At the end of the day, they finally slogged in to the assembly area just north of the small town of Baulny.

Stephen reported immediately to Colonel Harker, who had his

headquarters set up in a small stone farmhouse near the crushed gravel road paved by the French army.

He saluted Major Mabry, who led him into a small dining room, where Colonel Harker had set up his headquarters. He saluted the Colonel, who had mud all over his uniform and boots.

"At ease, Captain. I have some news for you. Our 325th Regiment and most of the 82nd Division have been ordered in reserve for support of the next attack.

"The new attack by the Fifth Corps will start tomorrow morning. The 82nd Division will be in reserve, ready to support the main attack if ordered.

"The offensive has not gone as planned, Stephen." Colonel Harker removed his helmet, and rubbed his forehead.

"One battalion from the 77th Division has even gotten surrounded by the Germans over at the Charlevaux Mill area. Germans have been seen from the air pouring down the road from around Cornay. This next round of attacks will be made to cut that road, and to cut off the Germans through the middle of the Argonne Forest."

"What are my orders, sir?"

"Your orders presently are to turn your Company 'I' over to Lieutenant Turner, because you have been promoted to the rank of major, effective October 1, 1918. Major Mabry, please pin these oak leaves on the new major."

"It would be an honor, sir."

Major Mabry removed the bars from Stephen's shoulder straps, and then pinned a gold oak leaf on each of his shoulder straps.

"Another thing, Stephen. For your conspicuous gallantry in action in the St. Mihiel Sector, General Pershing has awarded you the Silver Star. Please pin that medal on the major's chest, if you will Major Mabry."

"It is an honor, sir."

Major Mabry pinned the Silver Star decoration on Stephen's chest, and shook his hand.

"Congratulations, Stephen."

"Thank you, sir."

Colonel Harker then began to give Stephen his new assignment. "You will go to the 2nd Battalion headquarters area, and take command of that battalion. Major Russell was killed yesterday, along with Sergeant Major Pendergrass.

"A German 77 mm shell got both of them. Sergeant Carl Sanders has been promoted to Sergeant Major, and will be reassigned to you as Battalion Sergeant Major. You are to give him these stripes."

Stephen took the Sergeant Major's stripes from Major Mabry.

"Thank you, sir."

"Oh, I am sure that Sergeant Sanders earned his promotion if he managed to keep up with you."

"He is a fine soldier and NCO, sir. He truly is."

"That is why he was recommended for promotion, Stephen. You will report back here tomorrow at 0900 for a briefing. In the meantime, you can get set up at your new headquarters. The Advanced Post Office has caught up with us again. I have some letters for you and for Sergeant Major Sanders. Here they are."

Stephen took a bundle of mail from Colonel Harker. "Thank you, sir."

"That is all Major. See you in the morning."

"Thank you again, sir."

Stephen saluted the officers, and left the farmhouse. He paused outside of a stone fence, and began to look through the mail.

He saw a letter from Loralie, and one from Annie and Millie. There were two letters from Sheila to Carl in the bundle as well. He stopped and opened the letter from the girls, and read through the two page letter quietly. He missed his girls dearly, and tears streamed down his cheeks as he resumed his walk to the Company "I" bivouac area.

Lieutenant Turner saluted him and noticed his oak leaves right away.

"Congratulations are in order, sir. You sure deserved to be promoted."

Stephen smiled. "Same to you, Lieutenant Turner. Son, you are now commanding Company 'I.' If you will, send for First Sergeant Sanders. I have some news for him as well."

"Yes, sir."

Lieutenant Turner saluted, and soon returned with First Sergeant Sanders.

"I heard that congratulations were in order for you, sir. Your promotion to major, and your Silver Star."

"There is another promotion yet to be awarded, Carl. You have been promoted to Battalion Sergeant Major. Son, if you will, have him pin these new stripes on his sleeve."

"Yes, sir. It will be an honor, sir."

"Carl, after you get done sewing your stripes on, you need to get your gear and return back with me. We have a new posting."

"Yes, sir. Right away, sir."

"I also have some letters to you from Sheila. Here they are."

"Thank you, major. Thank you for everything."

"You deserved the promotion, Carl. I'll see you over there at the Battalion headquarters in two hours."

"Yes, sir."

That night, after 2000 hours, Stephen reported to 2nd Battalion headquarters. Captain Joseph Steele was the temporary Battalion Commander, and he was elated that Stephen had been sent over to replace Major Russell. Captain Steele was born and raised in Macon, Georgia, and played baseball against Stephen's varsity Georgia team when he was a student at Mercer University.

"We saw you over at Hill 42, sir. We all thought you were larger than life, sir. We are all thrilled to have you command our battalion, sir."

"Those are kind words, Captain Steele. We will sack out at present, and all of the officers will report to Colonel Harker at 0900 hours in the morning for another briefing. Have you set up headquarters in this barn?"

"Yes, sir. Your table and chairs are in that stall, sir."

"Well, it will at least keep us out of the damp French weather.

Have the officers assemble here at 0800 hours in the morning."

"Yes, sir." Captain Steele saluted Stephen, and left the barn.

Stephen went over to his table, and turned up the kerosene lamp, and then got Loralie's letter out of his haversack.

He opened the envelope, removed his helmet, and began to read. After he read through her letter once, he began to sob, and the tears ran down his cheeks.

He took out his tablet, and his pencil, and began to compose a letter back to Loralie. He chose his words carefully, and he took his time, writing out a letter that truly poured out his heart onto the pages.

He placed the finished letter into an envelope and carefully addressed it, believing all the while that it might be the last letter he would get home to Loralie.

When he was finished, he spied Carl entering the barn, with his letter from Sheila in his hand.

"Sir, Sheila's gonna have a child sometime in December. I'm gonna be a papa!"

"Well, congratulations are still in order, Carl. Being a father is wonderful. There is nothing in the world like fatherhood. I wish you and Sheila nothing but joy. On a more serious note, Carl, I have written a letter and have addressed it to Loralie. In case I fall in the next battle, please see that she gets it. I would really appreciate it if you could do that for me."

"Yes, sir. I would be glad to do that for you, sir."

"Thank you. Let's get some sleep. We have an officer's call and a briefing at Colonel Harker's headquarters at 0900 hours in the morning."

"Yes, sir. I've got to write a letter or two for myself, sir, right now, if you don't mind."

"Go ahead. I'm gonna polish off this tin of cold corned beef and the rest of my coffee, and then I'm turning in. Good night, Sergeant Major."

"Good night, sir."

Carl saluted Stephen as he left the barn, and headed to his billet in the back of the barn to finish his letters to Sheila and Ned.

Stephen reached into his haversack, and took out his Bible, and turned to I Corinthians, and began to read as he finished his dinner in the old barn.

CHAPTER FOURTEEN

On October 4, 1918, the entire U.S. First Army launched an attack on the German lines from a front that extended from the Meuse River, almost to the Aisne River on the west.

The earlier attack on September 26th had netted the Americans several miles of territory and around 23,000 German prisoners. The Allied command did not accept that result, and a renewed attack was launched on October 4th.

Shortly after a new attack was commenced along the line, officers of the 82nd Division were summoned to a briefing by Colonel George C. Marshall, a staff officer from General Pershing's headquarters. The briefing took place at a large barn on the Baulny Road.

Colonel Marshall was dressed in a crisp new uniform, and he was standing in front of a large map of the sector. He began to address the officers in a crisp and deep voice:

"Gentleman, the entire 5th Corps is driving the Boche units back from the area of the Apremont Road. General Pershing has asked us to draw up a planned attack which will be designed to cut off the Boche forces, and to sever their road and rail communications in the Argonne Forest.

"The key position that must be carried is Hill 180, which is located just below the town of Cornay. The Germans have several observation and artillery posts there, along with many machine gun nests. Aerial photos indicate that Hill 180 is heavily fortified.

"It must be carried, though, because it commands the entire German line of communications in the Argonne Sector.

"We have drafted attack orders on a timetable for the entire 82nd Division. 'H-Hour' is planned for the morning of October 7th. You will jump off then.

"I have ordered several artillery battalions to assist you. The guns might knock out some Boche observation posts, but you will have to root the rest of them off of Hill 180."

Colonel Harker had some questions. "Where will the Division advance to for a jump off point, and what will be the line of march?"

Colonel Marshall picked up a black horse crop, and began to point at objects on the map.

"You will march your men north along the Baulny-Apremont road past Montrebeau, and through the Farm des Granges. Your jump off point is there.

"At the H-Hour, the entire 82nd Division will advance across and over Hill 180, with the forward objective being one and one half kilometers west to the Chevieres Road and the railroad line. You are to trap and destroy any and all German units in that sector.

"Headquarters is anticipating that you will strike the enemy a substantial blow at this key sector. Good luck and God speed, gentleman."

Colonel Harker then summoned the regiment's officers for an officer's call, where the marching orders were circulated by Major Mabry to all commanders.

They then gathered their gear, and the buglers sounded 'assembly'. Soon, the entire 82nd Division began the march north along the Baulny-Apremont Road.

They marched past the corpses of artillery mules and stray farm animals killed by artillery fire and poison gas. They heard the other soldiers of the Fifth Corps attacking the German positions to the west, and they saw the artillery firing at the Germans.

German shells soon fell back in reply, however, but their range was short of the line of march of the 82nd Division. They marched for four kilometers, and soon arrived at their bivouac area for the night.

Several 75mm guns from the 129th Field Artillery were brought up for close support, and Stephen helped the batteries get situated on the edge of a grove of apple trees.

On his way back from visiting with the artillerymen, Stephen finally took the time to write another letter to Loralie. He decided to write two letters for her, but the second letter to her had the highest priority, since he was about to lead his men into battle again:

October 5, 1918
Near Baulny, France

Mrs. Loralie Harris
Rt. 1 Box 42
Royston, Georgia

My Dear Loralie:

If you receive this letter in the near future, then you should know that I have not survived the upcoming battle. I received your letter recently, where you admitted that you had been unfaithful to me, and had broken your marriage vows to me.

I have been extremely angry at you for doing so, and have taken out my frustrations upon the German soldiers I have faced. I channeled my anger, and used it as a tool against our enemy. It has served me well.

You should know that I have not used the past few months as a means to disrupt our family life. I have served my country, and have watched brave young men die in the cause of freedom. The flag that you salute every day represents the blood and the sacrifice of those who gave their lives for our freedom. As you read this letter, you will know that I gave my life for our country, and for your freedom.

Tell Annie and Millie that I love them very much, and that I know that they will grow up to be outstanding young women. Tell Ned that I loved him like a father, even as much as my own father. Tell Carl that I loved him as I would my younger brother.

Now I must tell you that I forgive you. I have learned in the midst of this war to let go of my anger, and to realize that the sun rises and sets no matter what my outlook on life may be. The world is a much larger place than I have even realized, and my personal desires and happiness pales in importance to the mission I was sent to fulfill. I am an officer in the United States Army, and I have done nothing less than my duty.

I forgive you because my Heavenly Father requires me to forgive you of your sins, so He can forgive me of mine. You have asked God to forgive you and have sought redemption, and you have asked me the same. I forgive you, Loralie. You also should know that I still love you, even though you broke our marriage vows.

I die with your name upon my lips, and your memory embedded in my heart. You must know by now that you are the one true love of my life, but my life now is over.

Tell our son about me, raise him well, and send him my love daily. My deepest regret is that I will not live to raise him, or see him grown up to be a man. I can only hope and pray that one day all of us will meet as a family in the Kingdom of Heaven.

Your Loving Husband,

Stephen

Stephen carefully folded the letter, placed it into an envelope, and pushed the envelope into his tunic pocket.

He went to his cot, and pulled off his trench boots and his helmet. He was asleep thirty minutes later, as the big German guns boomed from behind Hill 180.

The morning of October 7th was cloudy and misty, but the men went over the top and on the attack at 0800 hours. The entire 82nd Division began to attack Hill 180 from the east, and began the push up the heavily wooded foothill.

Stephen's battalion moved out as ordered, and soon encountered German machine gun fire at the base of the ridge. The hill was heavily wooded, with ravines and gulleys, making tank support difficult at best.

The machine gun nest commanded a broad field of fire, and Stephen heard bullets slamming into U.S. soldiers, and watched six men go down.

He used hand signals to tell his men to lie down, and he immediately began to crawl to a blown off beech tree. The tree had been cut in two by artillery fire, but stood five feet in height, with a forked branch in the middle.

Stephen used the stump for cover, as the Germans fired a burst his way. He chambered a .303 round in his rifle, and took aim at the gunner as he turned away to shoot the soldiers.

He fired, and the .303 round hit the gunner in the neck. As he slumped forward, his relief gunner reached for the machine gun. Stephen chambered a second .303 round and fired. At 120 yards, he cut the relief gunner's heart in half with the shot. The ammo man then reached for the weapon and Stephen shot him in the stomach.

The battalion then moved forward for an additional distance of a hundred yards, climbing Hill 180 in the process. A little further up the hill, they encountered another German machine gun nest manned by five men.

The Germans let them approach the hidden nest to within ninety yards, and then opened a devastating fire from their concealed position.

Sergeant Slater was cut in two by the deadly Spandau fire. Stephen ordered up a Stokes mortar platoon, who soon arrived with a three inch mortar. He ordered another platoon to pin down the gunner with rifle fire, while the mortar was assembled and set up. Once the mortar was set, he ordered the men to fire on the machine gun post, with full elevation.

He saw the Mark I high explosive shell, a gray shell with red stripes, as it was dropped down the tube. The shotgun cartridge on the shell hit the firing pin on the base cap, and the exploding cartridge ignited the propellant in the shell.

The shell arched out above them, and the U.S. soldiers dropped on their faces and waited. The round soon dropped on the German machine gun nest and exploded, killing all of the five man crew.

Stephen ordered an advance, and they soon had another Spandau in their possession. As they threw out sandbags around the machine gun post, a private fell face forward, after being shot in the back. Stephen heard gunfire from a tunnel leading into the hill.

He quickly yelled for the men to step away from the tunnel, and he pulled the pin on a grenade, and tossed it into the tunnel. It exploded directly, and he could hear screams from the Boche soldiers inside. As they emerged into the daylight, coughing and brushing their eyes, Stephen began to shoot them with his Colt .45 pistol, dropping eight men. The last two German soldiers threw down their weapons and surrendered. They were then herded down the hill, with their hands behind their heads.

Stephen took a pull from his canteen, and ordered his battalion up the wooded slope of Hill 180. They were two thirds of the way to the top of the hill, when they took fire again from a hidden machine gun post. Stephen ordered Company "E" to crawl forward, and to put a flanking fire on the machine gun post. The soldiers were well trained, and used the hilly and wooded terrain to their advantage, killing the German machine gunners, and the regular soldiers in the trenches that surrounded the machine gun post.

Twenty minutes later, the German firing stopped, and the Germans raised their hands, and began to file out of their trenches. They also began to march down the hill, with their hands behind their heads.

Lieutenant Tim Greene ordered his Company "D" to accept the surrender of the German troops, and they arose to accept their surrender.

When they got within 100 meters of the trench line, the Germans jumped back into their trenches, and the gunners began firing at American soldiers who were standing out in the open. Twenty American doughboys were immediately gunned down.

Stephen saw the Germans as they recommenced their firing. He grabbed a Stokes mortar, took out a Mark I shell, and pulled the tube up between his legs. He dropped the shell down the tube, and he then pulled the pin on another shell and fired it at the German trench.

The first German machine gun post was immediately destroyed, but the second post continued with a devastating fire that kept Stephen's men pinned down. Stephen ordered the men to crawl forward. As some soldiers were hit and killed, Stephen and Sergeant Sanders crawled forward on their elbows, until they found a sizeable pine tree log lying across a ravine.

The ravine provided them with a five foot drop, which was a effective defilade. Stephen ordered Carl to pull out his hand grenades, and whispered in his ear that the would throw their grenades at the German trench on the count of three.

Stephen and Carl pulled their grenade pins, counted to three, and hurled their grenades up at the German trench. The explosion killed four German soldiers, and temporarily silenced the machine gun.

Stephen immediately ran up the other side of the ravine, took aim at the machine gun post and fired at the gunner. The .303 round hit the gunner in the throat. Carl followed him, and fired a .303 round at the second gunner. His shot went through the second gunner's helmet.

Other German soldiers raced down the trench line, and began firing at them. Stephen calmly shot two German soldiers dead, while Mauser bullets whizzed past his shoulders.

The Stokes mortar crew began a steady rate of fire upon the German trench, killing seven more German soldiers.

Lieutenant Leon Roberts reported to Stephen with all of Company "F." Stephen ordered him to assault the German trench line.

Fifty German soldiers were massed between them and the top of the ridge, but they were hidden from Stephen's line of sight by a hedgerow.

They began to run forward, emboldened by their success, and they engaged the Germans in their trench. They began to shoot the Germans one by one, and they poured rifle fire into the German position. The Germans had engaged in an act of treachery by pretending to surrender. The Americans were there to make them pay. There would be no quarter this time.

A mortar shell exploded under the German machine gun post, and immediately killed the gunner. A second gunner pushed the dead German gunner out of the way, and then took control of the Maxim gun. Stephen and Carl hurried out of the ravine and chambered .303 rounds over the body of a dead German.

He did not take the time to aim his rifle at the gunner over 40 yards away, but fired his .303 Enfield by pointing the barrel at the gunner.

The .303 round caught the German gunner in the chest, and knocked him backward into his trench. Carl halted, and shot and killed the two ammo men as they attempted to get control of the Maxim gun.

Stephen looked behind him, and noticed that most of Lieutenant Tim Greene's platoon was running to catch up with him and Carl.

Stephen grabbed the Maxim gun, and turned it into the direction of the German trench. He pulled back on the bolt of the weapon, and began to fire at the Germans in their works. He began to mow the Germans down in succession. After he had shot twenty German soldiers with the machine gun, they began to throw down their weapons, threw up their hands, and surrendered.

Stephen stopped firing and ordered Lieutenant Greene's Company to herd the German prisoners to the rear.

Stephen asked Carl to continue up the German trench with him, as he thought that there was a German artillery observation post at a high point on the hill.

They walked another 100 meters, when Stephen saw a tall German officer talking on a telephone at the front of a large bunker.

Since the Germans had no artillery in place there, Stephen surmised that the forward observer had called in an artillery strike on their position.

He dropped to one knee, and fired a .303 round at the officer, striking him in the chest, knocking him down and away from the front of the bunker.

They began to walk toward the officer's position, when they heard artillery shells whirring and buzzing on a course that put the shells in their direction.

The German officer had obviously called in a strike on his own position. Stephen looked down the hill, and saw several companies and platoons of 82nd Division soldiers advancing to the crest of Hill 180.

He knew that counter battery fire was the only thing that could save a large number of American casualties.

He grabbed Carl by the shoulders, and told him to get down. They threw themselves into the ravine. Seconds later, two 88 mm shells impacted around the front of the German observation post.

Stephen took out his note pad, and began to write a dispatch to Sergeant Evans of the Signal Corps:

Capt. Sam Bachtal
Battery C 129th Field Artillery

Captain:

The Germans have several 88 mm guns in position near Cornay. They have zeroed in their fire at the crest of Hill 180. Hundreds of U.S. soldiers are converging on this point to capture this ridge as I write this note.

Urgently request immediate counterbattery fire 1 km south of Cornay at once. Map 14 Grid 20 Field 19, Coordinate G23.

Respectfully,

Major Stephen Harris
Commanding 2nd Battalion
325th Infantry Regiment

Stephen ordered Carl to run the dispatch down to Sergeant Evans of the Signal Corps. From there, it was to be sent down by carrier pigeon. There was not a moment to be lost.

Carl took the dispatch, and began to run back down Hill 180, in the direction of Sergeant Evan's last known position.

Stephen then climbed out of the ravine, and saw German soldiers emerging from the observation post. He began to shoot them with his Enfield .303. He shot five soldiers in the chest, as they each emerged from the bunker.

He then drew his pistol, and shot two German officers as they emerged from the tunnel at the front of the bunker. An 88 mm round exploded near the front of the bunker a few seconds later. A large piece of shrapnel from the shell flew in Stephen's direction.

As he heard the explosion, Stephen felt a red hot piece of metal fly through the left side of his chest. The shrapnel tore through his left lung.

He could not move forward, so he then eased himself into a sitting position on some sandbags in the trench, as 88 mm artillery shells landed around the top of Hill 180.

Carl found Sergeant Evans around 200 meters down the hill, and he sent Stephen's dispatch down on his favorite carrier pigeon, Cherie. Cherie was the fastest bird he had.

The forward headquarters post for the 129th Field Artillery had been set up near the 82nd Division Headquarters, and the Signal Corps station there was only two miles from the crest of Hill 180.

Cherie flew down at 35 miles per hour, and arrived quickly at the Signal Corps Station. Her message was quickly read to a forward artillery observer, who telephoned his 129th Field Artillery battery with the coordinates of the German guns.

Twenty minutes later, three 75 mm batteries nearby began to take the German 88 mm guns under fire. Twenty five minutes later, the German guns were dismounted, destroyed, and put out of action.

Carl trotted back up Hill 180 after the German 88 mm guns had been destroyed by the American batteries. He knew that Stephen's position had been taken under fire from the German guns, and he hoped that Stephen would be alive when he got there.

He advanced through the trench at the double quick, and then saw

Stephen seated on some sandbags.

He had blood all over the front of his uniform. "Oh sir, how bad are you hit? Let me get some help up here for you, sir. We can get you to an aid station."

Stephen was finding it more and more difficult to breathe. He took off his helmet, and asked Carl to get him some water. Carl gave him a sip of water from his canteen.

Stephen then grabbed his hand. "I took some metal from one of the German shells. Carl, I have two letters here for Loralie. Mail the last one I wrote to her. Destroy the first one I wrote to her. Send her my ID card, one of my dog tags, and my watch." Carl became upset.

"Oh, Stephen, please don't talk like that. I see some stretcher bearers coming this way now. Let them get you to an aid station. They can help you there."

Stephen knew that his time was running out, and he did not waste any time arguing with Carl.

"Tell your Papa that I loved him just as much as my own father. I love you just like a brother, too. Tell the girls and Loralie that I love them very much. Take care of my son when you get back to Royston."

The stretcher bearers had been sent for, and they soon had Stephen up on a stretcher.

"Tell Captain Steele to take command of the battalion. You need to report to him now, Sergeant Major. I'll see you a little later."

Carl took Stephen by the hand. "Yes, sir. You stay alive, sir." Carl then sent a corporal down the hill to find Captain Steele.

On the way down to the aid station, Stephen got out his pocket watch, and opened it up. He stared at the picture of Loralie and the girls, while the stretcher bearers walked with him down the hill.

He whispered to himself how much he loved all of them, including little Clayton, until it became too difficult for him to breathe.

Hill 180 was taken by the 82nd Division by the end of the day. Carl received permission from Captain Steele at dusk to go down to the aid station to check on Stephen.

He found the aid station at the base of the hill, but did not get there until after 2000 hours.

He found two Red Cross nurses there, and a doctor in a white coat attending to 300 soldiers, with the help of only ten orderlies.

When Carl made inquiry about Major Harris, the nurse advised him that Major Harris had died an hour ago. Carl then asked the nurse if he could please see the body, as he had some personal effects that he would need to send home to his family.

Carl found Stephen laid out at the rear of the aid station, with most of his uniform tunic cut away. His personal effects had been placed in an envelope which contained his name and rank.

Carl cut off one of Stephen's dog tags, and placed it into the envelope. He sat down on the ground beside his friend, placed his face into this hands, and wept like a child.

CHAPTER FIFTEEN

October 8, 1918
Near Cornay, France

Mr. Ned Sanders
RFD 1 Box 224
Royston, Georgia

Dear Papa:

It is with the deepest regret that I write you to inform you that Stephen was killed in action yesterday. We had just assaulted and had carried a German observation post, when Stephen was hit by a piece of metal from a German 88mm shell.

He died at the aid station at the front of the hill that we had captured. He told me just before he died that he loved me like a brother, and you just as much as his own father. I have some personal effects of his that I am enclosing, and ask that you please give them to Loralie. I also have a letter to Loralie that he wrote here a few days before he died.

Please get Pastor Amos Alexander, or an Army Chaplin from Camp Gordon, and have him go with you when you break the news to Loralie. Words cannot express my grief and my sorrow over Stephen's loss. They had already promoted him to Major, and he had won a Silver Star for what he did at St. Mihiel. They told me this morning that he had saved the lives of hundreds of 82nd Division soldiers, and he will be posthumously awarded the Distinguished Service Cross.

Please pray for me and the rest of this battalion, since we are the ones that will have to live our lives without him. We will finish this war, and we will finish the work that our Government sent us here to do. This will be the war to end all wars, I hope and pray.

Give Sheila my love, and tell Loralie and the girls that Stephen died at his post, doing his utmost duty for his country.

Your loving son,

Carl

On October 13, 1918, the American army captured Romagne in the Central Argonne. By October 23rd, the Americans had captured Grandpre and the Cunel Heights, and had completely driven the Germans from the Argonne Forest.

On November 1, 1918, the Americans completely broke the German lines on the Meuse River. The American attack was preceded by a firing of 36,000 rounds of mustard gas shells at the Germans, a high explosive artillery barrage, and the bombing of German lines by American aircraft. The roads and fields were soon strewn with dead Germans, horses, and destroyed artillery and equipment.

On November 5, 1918, the U.S. First Army was ordered to bypass Sedan, in order to give the French Fourth Army the honor of capturing it. Sedan was the site of the French defeat by Prussia in 1870.

On November 10, 1918, units of the 2nd and 89th Divisions of the U.S. First Army began to cross the Meuse River.

On November 9, 1918, facing mutiny by the navy, and revolution inside Germany, German negotiators were sent to Compiegne to negotiate an armistice. On November 10th, Germany accepted the Allied conditions for an armistice, and the Great War was scheduled to end on November 11, 1918, at 11:00 a.m. The eleventh hour of the eleventh day of the eleventh month, 1918.

On November 1, 1918, the War Department sent a telegram to Captain Charles Gunter, a chaplain at Camp Gordon, and ordered him to give a death message to the widow of Major Stephen Harris. He was ordered to travel to Royston, Georgia, and meet a Ned Sanders, who was a neighbor, and then to bring the tragic news of Major Harris' death to his family.

On November 2nd, Captain Gunter sent a telegram to Ned Sanders, asking him to meet him at the train station in Royston. Ned made a trip to the Royston Post Office as he got word that a certified mail parcel from France was waiting for him there. He drove down to the station after picking up the package, and Captain Gunter then briefed him on the reason for his visit. Ned pulled his GMC truck over on the side of the county road, and began to weep. He then opened the letter that Carl had sent him and wept even more. He then noticed that Stephen's Silver Star medal, his ID card, his watch, and his dog tag was included in the parcel Carl sent over.

Captain Gunter then told Ned that he had been sent to tell Loralie and her children about Stephen's death, and to give her Stephen's Distinguished Service Cross that he was posthumously awarded for 'distinguished gallantry and intrepidity' in action on Hill 180 on October 17, 1918.

Captain Gunter also showed Ned a tri-folded U.S. flag that he had been ordered to present to Loralie on behalf of a grateful War Department.

Ned regained his composure, and resumed his drive to Loralie's farm. When they arrived at the farmhouse at ten a.m., they saw Loralie on the front porch churning butter.

When Ned stepped out of the truck, she then saw that he had a parcel in his hand. When she saw an Army captain step out of the GMC truck with a folded flag in his hands, she covered her face with her apron, and fell down onto the porch, and wept hysterically.

END OF BOOK ONE

EPILOGUE

The Great Crusade

Early in the morning of June 6, 1944, hundreds of Dakota C-47 transport planes flew across the English Channel, and over into German occupied France.

Captain Matthew Clayton Harris sat in the back of the C-47, on a crude wooden bench, with his head pointed in the direction of the service door of the aircraft. The door was partially open, and as the plane flew over the English Channel, Clayton saw a vast armada of over 6000 Allied warships that were steaming toward the Normandy Coast. The enormity of the day's task was evidenced by the numbers of Allied ships dispatched to the French coast.

Underneath the aircraft, as the plane began to fly over France, small explosions could be heard from German AA fire on the ground. The AA was somewhat intense, causing the C-47 to buffet and wobble as the pilot fought to keep control of the aircraft.

Clayton looked out the service door, and saw a few large explosions off in the distance, a sign that some of the German AA fire had struck and brought down a C-47 transport loaded with paratroopers.

Clayton graduated West Point in 1939. He received his appointment from Milledgeville Congressman Carl Vinson, who was a distant relative of Carl Sanders, his father-in-law. When Clayton's father was killed in World War I, he won the Distinguished Service Cross. His father's service record paved the way for Clayton's appointment to the U.S. Military Academy. After his graduation and commission as a second lieutenant, Clayton went to jump school in Fort Benning to train as a paratrooper.

He was promoted to first lieutenant, and was sent to Camp Clairborne, Louisiana after war was declared.

His 82nd Division was transferred to Fort Bragg, North Carolina, where he completed his combat training. He was assigned there to the 505th parachute infantry regiment, Company "D."

He had seen action earlier in the war, in July of 1943, when his regiment parachuted into Sicily. Because of his ability in leading his platoon in Sicily and in Italy, Clayton was promoted to the rank of captain, and was given command of Company "D."

Now he was a part of a much larger invasion, the largest seaborne invasion in history, Operation OVERLORD. According to a message from General Dwight D. Eisenhower, their Supreme Commander, Clayton was part of a great crusade to rid Europe of the tyranny of Nazi Germany.

Seated in his Dakota transport, he was fully arrayed for the coming battle: He had hand grenades hooked to his harness, chocolate D rations, a morphine syrette, a canteen and a bowie knife, an antitank mine, an M-1 Garrand Rifle, a .45 automatic pistol, a pencil, and an order book.

He began to talk to his First Sergeant, Marvin Potts, but he had to yell to be heard over the roar of the engines.

Sergeant Potts had a question for him, "Did you get your letter off to your wife last night, sir? I saw you working on it back at the barracks."

"Yes, Sergeant, I did. I told Lisa that I loved her, and I couldn't wait to come home and see her again." Lisa was a dark haired, blue eyed beauty from Royston that was Clayton's childhood sweetheart.

Sergeant Potts wanted to talk about subjects unrelated to the war, so he asked Clayton more questions. "You were always real close to her anyway, weren't you, sir?"

"That's right. Her father and my father were close friends. Her father was my father's first sergeant in France. Dad was killed over in the Argonne Forest, but my father in law made it back home."

Sergeant Potts was a bit presumptuous. "Is that why you are such a terrific soldier, sir? Because of your father's sacrifice?"

Clayton did not know how to answer. He had always wanted to be a soldier. He had even gone against the wishes of his mother when he told her that he was enrolling at West Point.

Instead, he paid attention to the business at hand. "Sergeant, I am the jumpmaster, and you are on the port side of the plane, remember? We have a yellow light. Starboard side troopers, stand and hook on your parachute lines to the overhead cable. Port side, stand and do the same. See you in France, First Sergeant Potts." The troopers stood up, and hooked their parachute lines onto the static lines above them. The green light came on, and Clayton stepped near the open door. "Geronimo!" Clayton shouted, as he hurled into the rapidly moving air some 1000 feet above Normandy. Clayton looked up, and saw the trooper's parachutes deploying in a line behind the Dakota C-47 aircraft. His chute canopy deployed properly, and he began to float down into occupied France.

He felt the chute jerked him upward, and he slowly floated down into an apple orchard. He maneuvered the chute to miss a large apple tree, and soon landed hard. He dropped his rifle, and freed himself from the harness.

Gathering his chute with his left hand, he hid his jump gear under some hay. All around the orchard, he could hear the click-clacking of dime store crickets. One click-clack was to be answered by two, the recognition signal.

His company began to gradually assemble at their rally point, which was a swamp near the town of St. Mere Eglise. The members of the 82nd Division, unlike the 101st, had been dropped near their designated drop area. Their primary duty was to block the Cherbourg-Carentan Road, and to prevent a German direct attack on Utah Beach.

Clayton recognized the landmarks he had studied near the rally point, and he soon had his Company "D" on the road toward St. Mere Eglise. The small village must be captured and held, or the Germans could assault the Allies directly on Utah Beach.

Clayton looked at his map, and noted that the first objective was the bridge over the Merderet River.

They moved through a small field and a hedgerow, when they heard a truck moving in their direction. Clayton used hand signals to direct the men to take cover in the hedgerow, while Sergeant Mathers set up a 30 mm mortar, and Corporal Franks set up the .30 caliber machine gun at the end of the hedgerow.

Clayton knelt down near the end of the hedgerow, and soon felt a small, prickly animal bump into his hand. It was a hedgehog, and the animal scurried off into the field.

As the truck rounded the bend in the road near the field, Clayton saw that the vehicle was full of German troops. He raised his M-1 Carbine, and fired a round through the windshield of the truck, killing the driver. The rest of the company opened fire on the vehicle, sending dead and wounded soldiers off the side body of the truck.

A direct hit on the fuel tank by the machine gun caused the truck to explode. As the rest of the Germans ran away from the fiery wreckage of the truck, the American paratroopers cut them down with rifle and machine gun fire.

They were in a good defensive position near the road, but their orders were to secure the Merderet River bridge below St. Mere Eglise. Clayton ordered Sergeant Marvin Potts to get the men up and moving, as he checked his compass bearings by the light of the burning truck.

"We are three kilometers from our objective, Marvin. Have the men saddle up and move out."

"Yes, sir."

They began to march past a small paddock, and soon encountered a stone farmhouse a thousand yards down the road.

A pretty brown haired girl saw the American paratroopers, and she came out and kissed Corporal Walker on the cheek. Sergeant Potts tried to question the girl about the location of the German troops. He asked her "Boche?" He began to point in different directions. The girl, whose name was Brigid, pointed to the northeast and held up five fingers.

Clayton then began to question her. "Five kilometers?" Brigid nodded her head in reply. Clayton thanked the girl, and First Sergeant Potts gave her a chocolate D ration bar.

As they marched off, Clayton ordered the men to spread out, and move in the direction of the river.

Near a grove of beech trees, they encountered a small German patrol. The Germans opened fire on the company with machine pistols. Clayton heard bullets zing past his ear. Clayton dropped to one knee, and fired two rounds from his M-1 at the German patrol. Two Germans pitched over. Ten more men from the company opened fire, and the small German patrol was destroyed.

They searched the dead Germans for maps and papers, and found nothing but food in their knapsacks. They began to march in the direction of a swamp of alder trees. Clayton stopped the company, and ordered First Sergeant Potts to take five men and find a ford across the swamp.

"If you run into any Allied troops, use your dime store clickers for identification."

"Yes, sir."

"Move out."

The troopers spread out, and began to wade across the alder swamp that emptied into the Merderet River.

The Germans had blown up some of the dikes on many of the swampy creeks in the area, to flood fields across the Cotentin Peninsula. The major roads running from the beaches and back to St. Lo were on causeways above the flooded fields. The German defenses covered those causeways.

Clayton ordered Corporal Franks to set up his .30 caliber machine gun in a defensive position on the edge of the swamp.

Forty minutes later, Sergeant Potts returned to make his report. He was breathing hard.

"Sir, we found that the swamp empties into a creek a half a kilometer west of here. There is a large field and a hedgerow on the other side. I sent Wildcat McConnell up a tree, and he could see St. Mere Eglise on fire, sir."

"Very good, sergeant. Give the order to move out. I'm expecting the Germans to start moving out once the naval bombardment commences."

"Yes, sir."

They packed up their weapons and ammo, and began to walk downstream, until the swamp narrowed, and formed a large creek.

They soon crossed the creek, and then spread out into a large field. They soon heard the droning of C-47 transports, and the steady booms of AA fire from positions north of the town.

They heard C-47s droning in their direction, and they hurried to get out of the field. The troops scurried to the edge of a hedgerow, and they soon spotted the vertical stripes on the wings of an American glider as it swung down for a landing in the hundred acre field. The field had been used to grow hay, and the new grass there was short, making it a good landing zone.

Clayton acted at once. "Sergeant Potts, send a squad near that glider, and give them the recognition signal."

"Yes, sir."

As Sergeant Potts and his squad moved off to approach the glider, another glider began to land on the edge of the field. It came to rest a hundred yards from their position. Clayton sent Corporal Ivy and a squad of men to approach the near glider.

They soon heard a C-47 approaching very low and very fast. They caught a glimpse of the striped wings of a glider, but noticed that its angle was too steep. Clayton heard the glider as it crash landed near the hedgerow, two hundred yards away. He heard a cracking sound, as wood from the frame of the glider broke apart.

He sent for Sergeant Meadows. "Take Doc Hand down to that glider, and see if you can find a way to help any of their wounded."

"Yes, sir. Can I take Private Mitchell and Corporal Talton, sir?"

"Yes, sergeant, but get moving. This crash may have alerted the Germans."

Clayton was soon approached in the darkness by a major in the 325th GIR.

He saluted the major. "Clayton Harris, Captain, Dog Company, 505th PIR. I am at your disposal, sir."

"Hank O'Neal, 2nd Battalion, 325th Glider Regiment. It appears we only have two thirds of a company here, 'cause one of our gliders just broke up."

"I have sent a medic and some men down to check on them, sir. We are off of our drop zone by three kilometers. We shot up some

Germans between here and our drop zone. We have just located our objective near the town of St. Mere Eglise, sir."

"Very good. I will have my men retrieve their bazookas and anti-tank mines. We also have some mortars, and a little C-4."

Corporal Talton reported in to Clayton a few minutes later. "I'm afraid all of the men in the glider that cracked up are dead, sir."

Major O'Neal wasted little time. "I'll send some of my men back with you over there to get some bazookas and a couple of machine guns and some extra ammo. I'm sure those poor men won't mind us borrowing from them now."

Major O'Neal summoned his first sergeant, a Craig Reynolds from St. Louis, and ordered him to pick up the weapons and any extra ammunition from the crashed glider.

They soon moved out across the field, and down the road to a large stone bridge over the Merderet River near the town of St. Mere Eglise.

From a hill overlooking the river, Clayton could see a tall church burning in the town. They captured the bridge, and Clayton had volunteered to establish a defensive perimeter from a German counterattack.

Thirty caliber machine guns and 30mm mortars were placed on either side of the road, to cover the road from two different directions.

It was growing light out as Clayton checked his watch, and noted at 0530 hours, that a small yellow hue could be seen in the eastern sky. Soon a mighty invasion fleet of 6500 ships would be off Normandy, and naval gunfire would commence on the beaches at first light.

It was their job to keep these invasion routes open, and to repel any German counterattack.

Clayton had spied a dairy near the river, and he had sent several troops over to siphon gasoline from a truck there. The men also rounded up some rags and wine bottles from the dairy as well.

He then carefully constructed two Molotov cocktails to use against German tanks at the proper time. They soon encountered trouble of that sort at 0600 hours.

A Tiger tank and two platoons of German soldiers from the 91st Division were soon located by scouts from the 325th GIR. They relayed their signals to Major O'Neal, who sent a runner to Clayton to notify him of the German advance.

Clayton had briefed his men on the ammo and power of the Tiger tank, and he had trained his men to shoot their bazookas only at the metal tracks of the tank.

Bazooka shells were simply ineffective against the extremely heavy armor of the Tiger tank.

The tank soon appeared and began to take them under fire with its machine gun. When the tank closed to 60 yards, Clayton gave a hand signal to Corporal Watson and Sergeant Michaels to open fire at the tank's metal tracks. The two shells exploded, and one of the tank's metal tracks was completely severed.

The tank remained dangerous, though, with an 88mm gun, and a machine gun mounted on its turrett. Clayton ordered Sergeant Potts to grab a Molotov cocktail, and to follow him down the hedgerow, running in a crouch to avoid being spotted by the tank commander.

When they got to within ten yards of the crippled tank, Clayton and Sergeant Potts bent down and lit their rags they had sticking out of the gasoline bombs they had made from wine bottles.

Before the tank commander could fire upon them, they threw their homemade bombs at the turret of the crippled tank, and gasoline created fire engulfed the tank.

Once the fire got to the fuel tank of the Tiger, the tank exploded, as its ammunition blew up from the intense heat of the gasoline fire.

The American soldiers began to fire mortars and machine guns at the German soldiers, who now had no tank to hide behind. They took cover in the hedgerow near the road, and began firing at the Americans from there.

Several mortar rounds were fired into the hedgerow, and the Germans took casualties and retreated.

Clayton could then hear the naval gunfire on Utah and Omaha beaches, and he then realized that the landings were underway.

The burning Tiger blocked the road, and any other vehicle would be required to bypass the burning hulk, or push it out of the way. Forty minutes later, another Tiger tank and a company of German soldiers could be seen moving down the road.

The defensive perimeter was set up at right angles to a hedgerow, which was almost parallel to the road. The hedgerow was made up of a bottom layer of piled stones and earth, and a top layer of living hedge, which served as a fence in medieval times.

Now it provided the paratroopers and glider troops with cover. The troopers of the 505th set up a line of foxholes at right angles to the hedgerow. Clayton ordered .30 caliber machine guns and the 30 and 60mm mortars set up at intervals along the line.

Clayton ran over to confer with Major O'Neal at the last moment. "Sir, I have briefed my men that the bazookas can only damage the Tiger tanks by knocking off a track, or by hitting the underside of the vehicle. I believe the anti-tank mines would do the same, sir."

"I had some of my men put some anti-tank mines in the road. The bazookas can knock out their halftracks, I believe, captain. Did you have that experience in Sicily?"

"Yes, sir. We killed several Kraut half tracks in Sicily."

"Well, I see two companies of German infantry coming across the field, along with two halftracks. The Tiger tank is moving up the road. Have your men open fire upon the enemy when he closes to one hundred yards."

"Yes, sir. I'll get back to my company now, sir." Clayton saluted, and sprinted back to his foxhole.

The sound of the naval gunfire indicated that Allied troops were landing on the beaches at Normandy. The sun began to rise, and Clayton could make out the coal scuttle helmets on the troops as they closed the range.

At one hundred yards, Clayton gave the order to fire, and all of the troopers and glider troops opened fire upon the Germans with machine guns, M-1 rifles, BARs, and mortar fire.

The machine gunners on the half tracks began to return fire, hitting several troopers. The bazookas then opened fire on the halftracks from two directions, blowing them up, and stopping their forward progress.

Troopers cut down the Germans exiting from their half tracks with automatic weapons fire. The .30 caliber machine guns and the BAR men shot up the fleeing German soldiers, as they ran from their burning halftracks.

The Tiger tank continued up the road, and began to fire its machine gun into the hedgerow.

Clayton then heard an explosion, as the tank drove over several anti-tank mines. The explosions ripped through the tracks and underbelly of the Tiger tank. The track on the right side was blown clean off.

Molotov cocktails were again produced, and soon the second Tiger tank was set on fire.

The tank commander managed to climb out and surrender. He was only slightly burned on his hands and arms. He advised the troopers that his other crew members had been killed by the mine.

A third attack was made on the position later that evening, but it was easily beaten off. On June 9th, the Germans launched a heavier attack with the 91st Infantry Division, and several Tiger tanks. Clayton thought that the last attack would break through, but P-47 Thunderbolt aircraft bombed the tanks, and attacked them with rockets.

With the tanks knocked out of action, the men of the 505th and 325th Regiments held off the attacking German troops.

At the end of the day on June 12, 1944, the Allied troops had advanced as far as Carentan and Caumont in Normandy. The Allied beachhead was secure, and the Allies were in a position to advance deeper into France.

Annie Harris Greathouse was the tax assessor for Franklin County. She and her husband Ralph lived in Carnesville, where their son, Michael, attended Franklin County High School.

Michael worked during the summer at his father's dry goods store in Carnesville. On the morning of June 7, 1944, Annie arose as usual and cooked a breakfast at six a.m consisting of bacon, eggs, biscuits, grits, and coffee.

She cleaned up the kitchen afterward, and then began to dress for work. Ralph and Michael were already dressed, and they piled into Ralph's 1941 Chevrolet, and left to go downtown to open up the store.

Annie cut on the radio, as was her usual habit, while she dressed and brushed her hair. Edward R. Murrow interrupted the usual CBS Radio programming to make a special announcement.

Annie ran over to her bureau, and turned up the volume on her Dumont radio.

"The Allied forces have launched an invasion of the Normandy Coast in France. I read you now the order of the day from Supreme Commander Dwight D. Eisenhower to the Allied Expeditionary Forces. 'May God be with each of you fine soldiers. Soldiers, Sailors and Airmen of the Allied Expeditionary Force! You are about to embark upon the Great Crusade, toward which we have striven these many months. The eyes of the world are upon you ... Good luck! And let us all beseech the blessing of Almighty God upon this great and noble undertaking!'"

Murrow began to describe the size and scope of the invasion, but the facts and numbers got lost in Annie's head as she thought about her little brother, who most certainly would be fighting in Normandy by now.

It was the most crucial battle of the war, and it was happening right at this very moment. She ran over to her desk, and found her small notebook with telephone numbers, and called Roberson's Lumber Yard in Carnesville.

Clayton's wife, Lisa, was employed there as a secretary, and she wanted her to know that the invasion of France had begun.

She found the telephone number to the lumber yard, and asked the operator to connect her.

Lisa generally arrived for her shift at 7 a.m. She answered on the second ring.

"Lisa, hey it's Annie. I had the radio on after breakfast this morning, and Edward R. Murrow announced the Allied invasion of France this morning."

Lisa had not yet heard the news. She was excited about the invasion news as an American, but she was also concerned about the safety of her husband. "I have not turned on the radio yet today. I don't have a radio in my car. God, I hope that Clayton and his men are OK. I know they would have jumped behind the German lines before they invaded from the sea. All we can do now is pray for him and pray that our boys will win this fight."

"I know you are an optimist Lisa, but I just can't help but think about poor papa."

"Pa told me how great a soldier he was. He was his best friend, but he told me that he never exaggerated about the things your Papa did over in France. All we can do now is pray. You might want to call Millie. And maybe even Lori, too, for that matter."

"You know that I haven't spoken to mom in over a year. I will call Millie, though. We'll be down to see you on Sunday. You take care of yourself."

"You, too."

She ran over to her desk, and then looked up Millie's number in Athens, and asked the operator to connect her. Millie's school term had recessed at the end of May, and Millie was not an early riser.

She should be home. She answered the telephone on the second ring. "Hello."

"Millie. Hey, it's me. Have you heard the news on the radio this morning?"

"No, I just had breakfast. I'm taking the kids over to the library at the University this morning. What's up?"

"The Allies have invaded France, on the Normandy Coast, yesterday. Clayton should be in action over there right now."

"Oh God. I hope and pray that he will be alright. I can't help but think of poor papa, and the last time we saw him at the train station in Elberton. Does Lisa know about this?"

"Yeah, I called her as soon as I heard."

"What about mom?"

"I'll let you call her, if you want to. I'm not speaking to her, yet."

"What exactly is your problem with mom? She does miss seeing you."

"Do you really want to know the truth?"

"Yeah, I really do."

"Well, last year, Ned got the flu, and I went over to take care of him 'cause Sheila was sick, too. Anyway, while he was feverish, he started talking about a letter he had to write to Papa, where he had to tell him that there was an affair between Mom and a young railroad engineer, and the paternity of Clayton was at issue."

Millie did not immediately respond.

"Millie, are you there?"

"You know, Annie, it does not make sense. She started dating Mark not even six months after Papa was killed in France. We don't need to let this get out, though. Some skeletons should be left in the closet."

"I agree. And right now, anyway, we need to be Lisa's biggest cheerleaders. After all, our little brother is fighting over in France."

"Sure. You want to go to Carl and Ned's for Sunday dinner?"

"I have already told Lisa that we are coming. I'll call Sheila this afternoon. Say hello to George and Suzie for me."

"You bet. See you on Sunday."

Annie got ready for work, and soon got into her Model A Ford truck, and drove down to the courthouse to work at her office in Carnesville.

The following Sunday was observed by the Harris family daughters as a day for an annual family reunion. It would have been Stephen's 61st birthday.

Ned was now a spry old man of 78 years. He got up every morning at the dairy, and saw that the cows were driven into the milking stations and milked with the electric machine.

He continued to operate tractors and farm equipment to help Carl with hay baling and planting at the dairy farm.

Sheila and Carl continued to run the dairy. Sheila was 45 years old, but continued to sport her girlish looks and lovely figure. Carl remained thin and tanned, a product of his life of hard work on the dairy.

They had spent an entire day barbequing a small pig on a grate they had placed over an open pit of coals. The grate was set over concrete blocks stacked around the barbeque pit.

They propped roofing tin over the pig to keep in the smoke, and they shoveled coals into the pit periodically to cook the pig whole.

Sheila spent most of the Saturday making Brunswick Stew from parts of the pig, a roasted chicken, tomatoes, vegetables, ketchup, and Louisiana hot sauce.

Her daughter Lisa came over after work on Friday to help her cook vegetables and bake corn bread for their Sunday dinner.

Annie and Millie could be counted on to bring a dessert and a case of Coca Cola. Loralie normally baked a chocolate cake every year, because chocolate cake was Stephen's favorite.

The next Sunday, Annie and Ralph and Michael drove down in Ralph's '41 Chevy, and they brought a casserole dish of macaroni and cheese, and a case of Coca Cola in the small bottles. Ralph saved his gasoline coupons for two months to get the gas needed to take them over to Royston and back.

When they arrived at Ned's dairy farm, they saw Millie and Grace and Robert as they drove up in Millie's 1939 Cadillac.

Michael wondered why Dr. Westmoreland did not come with them. Annie told him why. "The Navy drafted him last month. He caught a train for Bethesda, Maryland two weeks ago. Your Aunt Millie will be on her own for a while. Go and help her get the fried chicken and those deviled eggs out of her car."

Michael obeyed his mother, and helped his aunt bring the food she had prepared out back to a large picnic table. Carl constructed the table several years before, after the family reunion had become an annual event.

Sheila began to carry some of her vegetables out to the table, and Michael soon began to help her as well. Lisa brought out a large tray of ham sandwiches, and a jug of iced tea.

Loralie soon arrived with a large chocolate cake. She had aged somewhat gracefully, with a full figure, and sparkling green eyes. Dressed in a yellow dress and a white hat, she sat the fabulous cake on the end of the large picnic table.

Carl was the first to congratulate her on her annual masterpiece. "It's beautiful, Lori. It looks even better than last year. Mark couldn't make it over for dinner today?"

Lori shook her head. "No, he had to pull a munitions train over to Charleston. He won't be back until tomorrow."

"Tell him that Sheila and I missed him, and we hope to see him soon."

"Thank you, Carl. Have you heard any news from France?"

"The Allies have established a beachhead in Normandy. They have not been thrown into the sea. I hope they can move out of there quickly, and get to Paris."

Michael was throwing a baseball around with his cousin Jason, when Ned came out of the house, and rang the large brass bell in the back yard.

"It's time to eat dinner, and I would just like to return thanks. But before we say grace, and eat this fabulous meal, I want us to remember Stephen, and the things that he stood for. I want Carl to come up here and tell us what kind of soldier he was, 'cause most of you know what kind of a man he was. Carl, come up and tell us about Stephen, if you will."

Carl took his hands out of the pockets of his overalls, and walked to the head of the table. His face turned slightly red, and his eyes began to water. He cleared his throat, and began to speak slowly.

"Stephen ... was the finest combat officer I have ever seen. When we were battling it out with the Germans, he was just larger than life. He could shoot and kill machine gunners with his rifle from any angle. He could use a mortar and kill the enemy. I saw him kill a German soldier with a shovel, when he ran out of ammunition. He was a ferocious man in battle. It seemed that his heart could just pump faster than ours in the heat of battle, and he never missed a lick. He was always thinking how he could destroy the enemy, in every type of situation.

On Hill 42, we got jumped by Storm Troopers, who attacked us with flame throwers. Any other officer would have panicked in that situation. We saw three men burned to death at once. Stephen just shot their tanks on their backs, and blew them up. He ordered us to do the same, and we eliminated the threat. We captured that hill, and for that, Division awarded him the Silver Star.

He could attack and destroy an enemy position with amazing skill. He knew the lay of the land, and would use the terrain to his advantage when he ordered an attack. When German guns got the range on us on Hill 180, he never flinched. He calmly sat under fire, and wrote out a message for the Signal Corps to order counterbattery fire on the German guns.

He died from a shrapnel wound from a German 88mm shell. I was not with him at the very end, and for that, I will always be sorry."

Carl broke down, and he took his handkerchief, and began to wipe the tears from his eyes.

Annie and Millie began to weep as well. Ned decided to delay the meal a few minutes, by changing the subject.

"Now Clayton is in the 82nd Division, a West Point trained officer. He and his men are somewhere in Normandy, fighting the Germans. Let us pray: Lord, we thank you today for the life of Stephen Harris. He was a good and a wonderful man, and he was a valiant and courageous soldier. Help all of us to cope with his loss, and help all of us to remember his devotion and his sacrifice for our freedom. Lord, this very hour, his son Clayton is in France fighting the Germans. We ask and pray that you will protect his life, Lord. Guard him with thy shield and thy sword. Make him invincible. Protect him and keep him from harm, as he fights to free Europe from the greatest tyranny yet known to this world. In the name of Jesus, Amen."

They then sat down to eat, and they began to pass food, vegetables, and bread around the large wooden table. After the delicious meal, they cut the chocolate pound cake that Loralie had baked. Loralie received many compliments on the job she had done with the chocolate cake.

"I had to save a lot of sugar ration coupons to get enough sugar to bake that cake."

After dessert, the women began to clear the table and wash the dishes. The men and the children broke out Stephen's old croquet set, and played croquet on the front lawn.

Millie and Annie began talking with Sheila while they were drying and putting the dishes away.

Millie was sullen. "Ned forgot to tell how awful we all felt when we saw Papa and Carl off at the station. You remember that Annie? We both thought that would be the last time we would see Papa, and it was. And then two years ago, we go to the same train station to see our little brother off to North Carolina. It was all too familiar."

"You need to be quiet, Millie. Lisa might just hear you."

Sheila peered out the kitchen window, and spied Loralie and Lisa on the swing under the Black Oak tree. "Relax Annie. I just saw Lisa talking to Lori out on the swing."

"I'm sorry, Sheila. We just both get emotional on Papa's birthday. We hated growing up without him. We both miss him a lot."

"I know you do. Mark did try to help you after he married Lori, though."

"Yeah, but he just wasn't our Papa. I know he meant well, but he could never replace Papa."

"I know. But we all must be strong for Lisa. She and Clayton have loved each other all of their lives. They were inseparable when they were children. They are deeply in love with one another. Please pray for her, that God may give her the strength to get through this war. I lived through it. So did Carl. Clayton is going to make it home yet, you just wait. You have got to have faith, Millie."

They continued to peer out the kitchen window at Lori and Lisa on the swing. They hoped that Lori had given Lisa a good pep talk about keeping the home fires burning. Millie was not in the mood to give such a talk. Annie thought her mother was nothing more than a hypocrite, but she was keeping those thoughts to herself.

On July 8th, Clayton received orders from SHAEF that the entire 82nd Airborne had been relieved. The 30th Infantry Division soon filed into their foxhole positions on the line in Normandy, and Clayton's company was ordered to march to the rear.

Clayton's "Dog"company had jumped into Normandy with 130 officers and men, and they returned back to the beachhead with 88 officers and men.

He was notified through Division that he was awarded the Silver Star for gallantry in action near St. Mere Eglise.

When they arrived at the pickup point near Utah Beach, they were fed a hot meal, and were treated to hot coffee and a shower.

At a small ceremony, General Matthew Ridgeway awarded several medals to the men of the 82nd Airborne. Clayton was the seventh soldier in the Division to be decorated.

The following day, "Dog" company marched out onto Utah Beach, and boarded an LST for England. On board the LST, the men were given hot coffee, and had steak and eggs for breakfast.

Clayton took a seat at the rear of the LST, ate his breakfast and finished his coffee, and began writing letters home to the parents of the men in "Dog" company that were killed in action in Normandy.

Once the LST docked in Southampton, they marched a short distance to a railroad, where they boarded the cars of a small train. On the way to their base at Ramsbridge, in south western England, Clayton penned a letter to Lisa, which he would post the following day at the base:

July 13, 1944

Mrs. Lisa Harris
RFD 1 Box 42
Royston, Georgia

My darling wife:
    We survived our jump into Normandy, and our hard fighting with the Germans. We were relieved at the front

three days ago, and are now on a train bound for our base in England.

The invasion has been a success, and the Allies are now lodged hard on the corner of France. We lost several men in our company to German action, and to accidents on the night of D-Day. Please tell mom and Annie and Millie that I am OK, and everything is fine with me at present.

All of us have matted hair, and we are all covered with dirt, sweat, dust and grime. This train smells of all our unwashed bodies, and we stink. Our first order of business when we get to the base is a series of hot showers, shaves, and our uniforms will get boiled and laundered.

Division did award me the Silver Star for what we did in Normandy, and we did our part there to help win the war. I am certain that they will call us to jump into France again, but now we must rest and refit.

I got your letter last month where you said that mom had deeded us Dad's home place for us to live in after the war. Go ahead and let Mrs. Tapp sign a month to month lease right away, as you can stay with your folks until I get home from the war. When I do get home, love, I plan to take you into my arms, and get started at making us a family to fill up our big house in the country. I long to hold you next to me, and to kiss your sweet lips again. The train is almost at the station, Lisa. I have to go now. I will write you again after we get to the base.

Your loving husband,

Clayton

Back at the base in England, promotions were handed out to some of the returning paratroopers. Clayton was promoted to the rank of major, and was given command of the second battalion of the 505th Parachute Infantry Regiment. They got paid, and the APO mail caught up with them, and Clayton received several letters from home.

The next month, the 505th was alerted, and was transported to Uppottery to the airfields to fly out for a jump into Holland.

The first time they were alerted, they were informed that a British Armored Division had overrun and captured their jump sites in Holland.

On September 15th, the entire 82nd Airborne Division was alerted, and once again was transported to Uppottery, where General James Gavin gave the officers a briefing.

The new mission was in support of Operation Market Garden. The 82nd Division was to parachute into Holland, and to seize bridges over the Maas and Waal Rivers, and to hold the high ground between Nijmegan and Groesbeek.

The Guards Armored Division of the British Army was to roll over all of the bridges held by the Allied airborne troops, and the plan was to cross the lower Rhine River into Germany.

The attack was to be the first daylight drop of the war, and would be the largest airborne assault yet made. 16,500 paratroopers and 3,500 glider troops consisting of the U.S. 82nd Division, the 101st Division, and the British 1st Division, were to seize bridges over a 60 mile long path into Germany. They were to hold the bridges for a crossing by British armored units into Germany.

Clayton and his battalion blackened their faces, packed their gear, and took off from Dakota C-47 transports from Uppottery airbase in England.

In October, Carl Sanders was in the process of getting in the last of his hay crop with his new John Deere tractor, when he saw Sheila waving at him from across the field.

He opened up the throttle on the tractor, and eased it into a higher gear, and soon pulled up to the field fence where Sheila was standing. She began waving a letter at him.

"Carl, you got a letter from Clayton. Please come in and read it to Ned. He wants you to read it to both of us."

Carl gladly complied, and he walked with Sheila across the yard and into the kitchen, where Ned sat waiting at the table with a pitcher of iced tea.

He poured Carl a glass and passed it to him. "Well son, we're waiting."

Carl chuckled, and opened the letter with his pocketknife. Some of the text had been edited by Army Censors, but Carl read what he could.

October 15, 1944
Near Nijmegen, Holland

Mr. Carl Sanders
RFD 1 Box 224
Royston, Georgia

Dear Carl,

We are here in the Netherlands near the Waal River firing artillery at the Germans here, who fire back at us with 88 mm guns. The warfare here is just like it was in World War I. It is static trench warfare. We shoot at them, they shoot back at us.

The rations here are supplied by the British, and they are just piss poor. The oxtail soup is practically lousy, it is just a thin greasy broth with bones floating in it. If it weren't for the fresh fruit and food we get from the civilians here, we all would starve to death.

We achieved all of our objectives when we dropped into Holland last month. The fighting was hard, but we captured both bridges over the Waal River, both here and at the town of Grave. What happened to us was also a problem with the 101st. The British could not get to their objectives fast enough, and the Germans counterattacked.

We killed over 200 Germans, and knocked out four tanks defending the bridge over the Waal River here. The first wave over the Waal in the first attack lost half of its men. We were in the second wave, and we fared better. Crossing a wide river with a ten knot current in a light assault boat is one hell of a trick to pull off. We did it though, and now we are here to stay.

The Germans have a new Tiger Royal tank that just knocks out anything we have. They shot their 88 mm guns on those things at the British Shermans and Cromwells, and they killed our tanks every time. We can only slow them down by shooting off their tracks with our bazookas.

The Market Garden Operation was supposed to end this war. Ike picked the wrong general to run the operation to win the war. General Montgomery and the British just don't have the moxie to pull off any offensive operation of any kind. This operation did not win the war. The Germans just had too much armor in this area to allow that.

It seems to me that Eisenhower has forgotten that he is an American general first and an Allied general second. He should put American and not British generals in charge of any offensive operations against the Germans. General Patton would have been a much better choice.

We are to be relieved here within the next week or so, and scuttlebutt says that we are to be relocated to nest camps near Rheims, France. I know that Dad's grave is near Romagne, and I am going to hire a French guide to take me there.

Once I get there, I will snap a picture of his grave, and

will send it home to you. Tell Sheila and Ned that I said hello, and give Lisa a hug and a kiss for me. I will write you all once I get to France.

Yours truly,
Clayton
Major, Commanding 1st Battalion
505th PIR

Carl looked up after reading the letter, and saw tears running down Ned's cheeks. He could not believe that the Army censors had left the paragraphs about General Montgomery intact. However, the censors were probably American soldiers, and they were also probably frustrated with General Montgomery as well.

Carl looked up, and saw that Ned had tears running down his cheeks.

"What's the matter, Pa?" He asked.

"Do you remember when Stephen wrote me after you broke the German lines in the St. Mihiel sector?"

"Yeah, I remember."

"Stephen wrote me then, and in his letter criticized General Pershing in just the same way as Clayton just criticized General Eisenhower."

"Yeah, I remember him talking about that. You're exactly right."

"Well, if you ever had any doubts about Clayton being Stephen's son, you can erase them all right now."

Carl took a swallow from his glass of iced tea. "You're right, Pa. You're exactly right."

"Let me see that letter, son. Maybe we can piece together what the government censors took out, and we might understand everything Clayton had to tell us."

"Here it is, Pa. You go ahead. I need to get in the rest of the hay."

Carl handed Ned the letter, and said a prayer to himself, giving thanks to God that Clayton remained alive and well in Holland.

On November 11, 1944, the 82nd Airborne was relieved, and the men were transported by trucks to Rheims, France. There, the division was billeted in rest camps. The following morning, Clayton went to General Gavin's headquarters, and arranged a 12 hour pass for himself and First Sergeant Potts. He then went to the motor pool and arranged for the use of a jeep.

Driving back to the camp, Clayton picked up First Sergeant Potts, and they began their drive over to the huge U.S. Cemetery near Romagne. General Gavin even loaned Clayton a camera, since he knew the real reason for Clayton's 12 hour pass.

On the way to Romagne, they picked up a French farmer named Claude Gerard. Claude agreed to serve as their guide for the day, in exchange for a couple of U.S. dollars, and a pack of cigarettes.

Claude gave them driving directions on the old road, showing them the proper turns to take along the way.

They finally arrived at the huge American cemetery just across the way from the highway. Clayton dismounted the jeep, and saw acres and acres of white stone crosses in neat rows and formal lines.

He began to walk on the edge of the cemetery, until he saw the word "Harris" on one of the crosses near the center of the Romagne Cemetery. He then knelt down and looked at his father's grave. The cross read:

Stephen W. Harris
Brevet Major 325th Infantry Regiment
U.S. Army
KIA October 7, 1918

Clayton began to weep. He never knew his father. He only remembered him from his photographs, and from what his mother and sisters, and Carl and Ned had told him.

Yet in north central France, he felt a kinship with his father. He was now a fellow comrade in arms, an officer in the United States Army. He pulled off one of his dog tags, and placed it around the top of the cross that served as Stephen's headstone.

Sergeant Potts saw Clayton in front of his father's headstone, and he retrieved the camera from the jeep and began to take pictures. After a half hour at the grave site, Clayton arose, and offered Claude five U.S. dollars for guiding them over to the American Cemetery.

Claude declined, telling Clayton that his father and thousands of Americans like him paid a price for his services many times over.

Clayton took Claude to a local café, and bought him a beer and a sandwich for his trouble anyway.

When they got back to the Command Post, Clayton had a friend in the intelligence section develop the photos from the cemetery.

Clayton then sat down and wrote a letter home to his mother, and enclosed one of the photos:

November 17, 1944
Near Rheims, France

Mrs. Loralie Lake
RFD 1 Box 53
Royston, Georgia

Dear Mother:
We have been transferred off the front lines to a rest camp near Rheims. Today, I got a jeep from the motor pool, and Sergeant Potts and I, and a Frenchman named Claude drove out to the American cemetery at Romagne.

I found father's grave there, at Plot C, Row 8, Grave No. 30. His tombstone is a white stone cross, which says:

Stephen W. Harris
Brevet Major 325th Infantry Regiment
U.S. Army
KIA October 7, 1918

Enclosed please find a photograph of me at the grave site. I never knew my father, and never had the opportunity to get to know him. Somehow though, I felt a bond with him as I sat at his grave site.

I know how hard it was for Annie and Millie to grow up without him, and if I had one wish right now, it would be that Dad had survived the war and returned home to us. Ned told me how tough it was to lose his wife in '99 when she gave birth to Carl. I can only imagine how tough it was for you to get word that Dad had been killed in action in France.

I hope to survive this war, and if I do, I will resign my commission, and return home to raise a family and work as an engineer. Please don't confuse my goal to leave the army as a knock against the Service. Only a strong and well trained military can keep us from having to fight such horrific wars as this one. We cannot depend on foreign alliances for our security. It can only be had by maintaining a professional army and air force and navy.

Say hello to Mark for me, and tell him that although I knew he wasn't my father, that I really appreciate the many things he did for me as a boy. I have to go now, mother. I have an inspection in ten minutes. Tell Millie and Annie that I will write them later, and tell Lisa that I love her.

Your loving son,

Clayton

On the 12th of December, 1944, Sheila and Lisa baked two large boxes of chocolate chip and sugar cookies for Clayton. Clayton had written all of them in November, and had requested a box of special goodies at Christmas time.

They took the cookies out of their gas stove and put them on racks to cool, while Carl wrote out a Christmas greeting card to Clayton.

The cookies were decorated later, and Carl wrapped the box

carefully with brown paper, and secured the box with strong kite cord. He addressed the parcel to Clayton, and took the package down to the post office in Royston the next day. As he mailed the package off, Carl hoped the war would soon be over.

All of the news reports had previously indicated that the Germans appeared to be beaten, and the war would be wrapped up in a matter of weeks.

Adolf Hitler and his Nazi regime reached down into their well of resources, and scraped together a potent armored force to throw at the Allied Western Front before Christmas.

In addition to tanks and artillery, a column of German paratroopers had been trained to disguise themselves as American MPs, and to change over road signs, and cut Allied communications behind the U.S. lines.

On December 16, 1944, the German Army launched a massive armored attack at the American lines in the Ardennes Forest of Belgium. Twenty-five divisions launched an attack in the Ardennes Forest in bad snowy weather, for the purpose of driving a large wedge in the American lines.

The German objective was the port at Antwerp, Belgium. The resulting attack by the Germans caused the largest single battle on the Western front in World War II.

Over 800 American tanks were destroyed, and two infantry divisions were destroyed. The first breakthrough was achieved in the lines held by the U.S. VIII Corps.

General Eisenhower immediately guessed the objective of the German threat, and issued orders from Rheims which resulted in the movement of large numbers of American troops to the front.

The 101st and 82nd Airborne Divisions were alerted on the 17th, and were trucked to weak points along the front lines.

The 101st Division was ordered to hold Bastogne, Belgium, and the 82nd Division was ordered to take up positions at Webermont, Belgium. On the 19th of December, the 82nd Division was moved to defensive positions on the Salm River.

The terrain was the dense Ardennes Forest, which consisted of pine trees, fir trees, and oak trees in a rugged, hilly terrain.

The major road and railroad junction was the town of St. Vith. The German plan of attack by the Fifth and Sixth Panzer Armies called for the capture of St. Vith by 1800 hours on December 17th.

The U.S. 7th Armored Division and the 291st Engineer Combat Battalion bore the brunt of the initial German attack at St. Vith.

The 82nd Airborne Division came to their aid, and the troopers were deployed in foxholes in the snow to bolster the lines held by the engineers and the 7th Armored Division. The fighting grew intense, as the troopers were put under attack by large numbers of German tanks and armored vehicles.

Clayton set up a forward artillery observer post at the front, and called in the coordinates of attacking German tanks by radio to the artillery units. The troopers dug foxholes, and set up a base of fire with their .30 caliber machine guns and 60 mm mortars.

Several guns from the 275th Armored Field Battalion had been relocated west of St. Vith. A plan of defense of Clayton's battalion was immediately sketched out with Clayton's officers and NCOs.

They would use machine gun and mortar fire to kill attacking Germans on foot. Bazookas would be used on the German Mark IV tanks only. The Tiger and Panther tanks would be dealt with only by the field artillery. The 155 and 105mm guns were heavy enough to knock out any tank, Tiger or otherwise.

Out in the snow, with no true winter gear on, Clayton had donned his woolen underwear, two sweaters, his battle dress fatigues, and a trench coat. It was still horribly cold, however.

The Germans soon launched a series of attacks from the direction of St. Vith. The American companies shot up a large patrol of Germans on foot as they approached their position. They used mortars and machine guns to destroy two German halftracks that attacked their position at 1800 hours on the 19th.

At dawn on the 20th, a large column of Tiger tanks was spotted by a scouting party, and their numbers were reported to Clayton.

He got on the radio, and cooly called in their coordinates to the 155mm batteries of the 275th Armored Field Battalion. Heavy fire soon came in, toppling trees, and destroying the tanks as they came in.

The next morning, a company of German soldiers attacked their position, with the support of a Mark IV tank. The soldiers were soon killed by machine gun and 60 mm mortar fire from the American troopers. The tank, though, began to advance on their position.

Clayton grabbed a bazooka, and ran to within 70 yards of the tank. He fired the bazooka at the base of the tank, near its belly.

At the same time, the tank fired a machine gun burst at Clayton. The bazooka round destroyed the tank, but two of the machine gun rounds struck Clayton in the left leg, shattering the bone in the tibia.

Clayton was pulled out by medics and placed on a stretcher. He was bandaged up, and given a syrette of morphine. On the way to the aid station, Clayton instructed First Sergeant Potts to tell Captain David Mock to take over command of the battalion. Clayton then passed out.

He awoke later at a field hospital near Brussels, where a doctor operated on this left leg, and placed it into a cast.

The next day, Clayton was loaded aboard a C-47 Dakota, and flown to the 192nd General Hospital near Oxford, England.

On December 23rd, the weather cleared, and Allied P-47s and P-51 Mustangs began to attack the German armor, and the German threat was stopped short of the Meuse River. Lt. Colonel Creighton Abrams' 37th Tank Battalion of General George Patton's Third Army broke through the German lines, and relieved the 101st Airborne at Bastogne on December 26, 1944.

The Allied troops then went over on a counterattack, and began to close down the wedge the Germans had driven into their lines. The Battle of the Bulge soon came to a close.

On January 14, 1945, Lisa went to work at the lumber yard, worried about Clayton, because she had not heard from him in almost six weeks.

She had listened to the CBS Radio broadcasts covering the Battle of the Bulge, and knew that a large battle had been fought in the Ardennes Forest in December.

As she worked on U. S. Government purchase orders at ten o'clock that morning, she was surprised by a Western Union courier, who handed her an envelope containing a telegram from the War Department.

She thanked the courier, and her heart went up in her throat as she opened the envelope and read the telegram:

WESTERN UNION
A. L. WILLIAMS
PRESIDENT

7.36 4 EXTRA GOVT = WVK WASHINGTON DC 13
1944 Jan. 14

VIA ATLANTA, GA

MS. LISA HARRIS =
ROYSTON =

REGRET TO INFORM YOU YOUR HUSBAND MAJOR MATTHEW CLAYTON HARRIS WAS ON DECEMBER 21ST 1944 WOUNDED IN ACTION IN BELGIUM UNDER GERMAN ATTACK PERIOD
YOU WILL BE ADVISED AS REPORTS OF CONDITION ARE RECEIVED =

J A ULIO THE ADJUTANT GENERAL

LISA

Lisa asked permission to make a long distance call to the War Department in Washington. She spoke to a Major McCoy at the War Department, who took her number and promised her a reply in two hours.

Sure enough, he called her back, and gave her the address of a hospital in England. She returned home late that afternoon, only to find a letter from Clayton waiting for her when she got there:

December 24, 1944
Near Oxford, England

Mrs. Lisa Harris
RFD 1 Box 224
Royston, Georgia

My Darling Wife:

I was wounded by machine gun fire from a German Mark IV tank on the 21st. They took me to an aid station and a field hospital, and then flew me over here to England.

The two machine gun bullets shattered the bones in my left leg, and they have it in a cast. I was unable to write you earlier, because they have had me on a lot of morphine. I am expected to recover, and will probably rejoin the battalion by May. I was informed by Division a couple of days ago that I will be awarded a Distinguished Service Cross.

I do not deserve this decoration, but the men under me deserve it ten times over. They were superb under fire, and they stopped the Germans cold at the Bulge.

We came over here to do a job, and our Division has performed brilliantly. The men are the finest troops I have ever seen anywhere. I know that they will go on and win this War. Our Army will never stop until Hitler and his evil regime are destroyed, and the war is totally won.

Enough about the war. After the war, darling, I will resign my commission, and come to work with an engineering firm in Toccoa.

Pat Patterson, who is a lieutenant in C Company, is a partner in the firm, and he has asked me to come to work with him and his dad after the war. I want us to move back into dad's old house, and let us get down to the business of starting a family and raising children. I love you, Lisa, and your love has taken me through the darkest and coldest nights one could ever imagine on a battlefield.

I did hear from my buddies in the battalion. They really enjoyed your cookies! I have to go now, I'm getting groggy from all this morphine. Maybe I'll do the nurses a favor and wet my bed again! Ha! Ha!

Your loving husband,
Clayton

In May of 1945, Nazi Germany was totally defeated by Allied and Soviet forces, and Germany signed an instrument of surrender. Clayton was transported to Fort Benning, Georgia, where he completed his rehabilitation and recovery from his wounds. He resigned his commission from the Army on August 3, 1945. He was given a ten percent disability to the left lower extremity.

He returned to Royston, and then accepted a job in an engineering firm in Toccoa. He set up house keeping with Lisa in his father's old house near Royston. He and his soul mate Lisa remained happily married the rest of their lives in Royston. There they raised two sons and a daughter.

Printed in the United States
26858LVS00002B/1-12